"Okay. Look. I didn't want to get into this, but . . . Alanna's missing," Conner said.

"Missing?" Tia repeated. "Like, gone?"

"Yeah," Conner said.

"You mean, she ran away?" Andy asked, widening his eyes. Conner nodded. "When?"

"Saturday, I guess. Her parents didn't notice until Sunday morning, so she probably left while they were asleep."

"Wow," Tia said. For once she seemed to be at a loss for words, which made it a perfect time to take off. Conner started to get into his car, but Tia stopped him.

"Wait a second," she said. "This is Monday—you can't skip your guitar lesson. You've got that audition on Wednesday. You need to practice."

Conner turned back to Tia and narrowed his eyes. Was she serious? How was he supposed to even think about anything else when Alanna was missing?

"I don't need to practice," he said evenly. "I need to find Alanna."

"Oh, come on, Conner," Tia said. "Don't be so dramatic. I'm sure she's fine. She's probably already home. But even if she isn't, you have to focus on your audition. You can't go running all over town looking for her. This audition could be a major part of your future."

His future, huh? What about Alanna's? Or didn't she deserve one?

Don't miss any of the books in Sweet Valley High Senior Year, an exciting series from Bantam Books!

Visit the Official Sweet Valley Web Site on the Internet at:

www.sweetvalley.com

Never Give Up

CREATED BY
FRANCINE PASCAL

BANTAM BOOKS
NEW YORK • TORONTO • LONDON • SYDNEY • AUCKLAND

RL: 6, AGES 012 AND UP

NEVER GIVE UP
A Bantam Book / April 2002

Sweet Valley High® is a registered trademark of Francine Pascal.
Conceived by Francine Pascal.
Cover photography by Michael Segal.

 Produced by 17th Street Productions,
an Alloy, Inc. company.
151 West 26th Street
New York, NY 10011.

ISBN: 0-553-49389-2

Visit us on the Web! www.randomhouse.com/teens

Published simultaneously in the United States and Canada

Bantam Books is an imprint of Random House Children's Books, a
division of Random House, Inc. BANTAM BOOKS and the rooster
colophon are registered trademarks of Random House, Inc. Bantam Books,
1540 Broadway, New York, New York 10036.

PRINTED IN THE UNITED STATES OF AMERICA

OPM   0 9 8 7 6 5 4 3 2 1

To Emma Marie Peckos

Alanna Feldman

My parents are control freaks. When I was six, they pushed me into this kindergarten for "gifted" kids, even though all my friends from preschool were going to the regular one. And if I wanted to go over to a friend's house, they'd check first to make sure it was one of the kids from my program because they didn't want me associating with the wrong crowd. The wrong crowd. In <u>kindergarten.</u> That was twelve years ago, and they've only gotten worse.

melissa Fox

Once—just once—I'd like to hear my mother ask me what's wrong and then wait for my answer. But it's never going to happen. I mean, it's not like I want to have some kind of close relationship with her or anything. That would be too much. But she's my mother. Shouldn't she be baking me cookies or hugging me and telling me everything's going to be all right? I don't think she's ever done either. She used to bring home a package of Oreos once a week, but I don't ever remember getting a hug that didn't feel stiff and forced. And when she does ask me what's wrong, I know exactly what she wants to hear. "Nothing." That way she and Dad can still go out to dinner, or to a play, or wherever it is they want to go. And they won't even be late.

Ken Matthews

I bet if I got into Harvard, my dad would say, "Harvard? Why do you want to go there? They don't even have a decent football team." And if I got into Notre Dame, he'd probably complain that they haven't won a title since Lou Holtz took them 12-0 in '88. Even if I'd taken that U. Mich. scholarship—like he wanted—he would have found some way to criticize me for it. It's crazy. I don't know what he wants from me or what he expects. All I know is that nothing I do is good enough. And it probably never will be.

Conner pulled Alanna closer as they swayed to the music. Alanna sighed happily, then closed her eyes and rested her head on his shoulder.

There was a band playing somewhere . . . or maybe it was just the radio. Not that it mattered. Alanna wasn't even sure where they were. At a club? In Conner's living room? No. There was definitely the feeling of being outside. A warm breeze. Salty air. There might even be stars.

Alanna started to open her eyes to look around, then decided she didn't care. She felt so warm and safe in Conner's arms that she didn't want to do anything to change it. In fact, if she could have, she would have melted into him and stayed there forever.

They danced for a while, turning in slow, small circles, until Conner pulled back slightly. Alanna raised her head to see him staring down at her and realized she could see her reflection in his gorgeous green eyes. Then his mouth curved gradually upward

1

into a smile, and when his lips parted, Alanna felt as though she knew exactly what he was about to say.

"Alanna!" Conner shouted.

It was such a shock that Alanna squeezed her eyes shut and twisted her shoulders away from him, but he was holding on to her tightly.

"Alanna!" he yelled again, but there was something different about his voice. Bewildered, Alanna forced herself to hold his gaze. She searched his eyes, trying to determine exactly why he was calling her name so loudly when she was right in front of him, but as she scrutinized his face, something strange happened. She realized he was beginning to fade away from her.

Alanna reached for his shoulders in an attempt to hold on to him, but she couldn't get a firm grip, and soon she found that she was grasping at nothing but air. She tried to yell his name, but her voice didn't come quickly enough. He was gone.

"Alanna Ellen Feldman!" Yet his voice was still there—although it still didn't sound quite right.

That was when it hit her. The screaming was real. The dance with Conner was not.

All at once Alanna became aware of sheets, blankets, the pillow beneath her head. She rolled onto her side and opened her eyes just enough to let a little light in, and slowly the rose-colored walls of her bedroom came into focus. Next she saw the off-white Berber carpet. Then finally—and regrettably—Alanna's eyes came to rest on the figure standing beside her bed. The one that was doing all the yelling. Her mother.

"Well? What do you have to say for yourself?" Mrs. Feldman demanded, hands on her hips.

"Oh, no," Alanna murmured, still reeling from the sudden transition between dream and reality.

"*Oh, no?*" her mother repeated. "Is that it? You skipped out on an important family function to go to a dance—deliberately disobeying your father and me—and all you can say is '*oh, no*'?"

Alanna rubbed her eyes and glanced at her mother. What a way to wake up.

"Well, I certainly hope you had a good time," Mrs. Feldman went on. "Because that's the last dance you'll be going to for a while."

Alanna propped herself up on her elbow. "What's that supposed to mean?" she asked.

"It means that I've had it with you, Alanna. And so has your father."

Alanna rolled her eyes. It was the start of another fun-filled weekend at the Feldman house.

"I mean it, Alanna," her mother continued. "Your little performance last night was the last straw."

Wearily Alanna sat up and swung her legs off the side of the bed. *The last straw.* She'd heard that from her parents before. Plenty of times. But what they didn't seem to understand was that she'd just about reached her limit with them too.

"What do you want me to do?" Alanna asked, cradling her head in her hands. It was an impossible question, she knew. No matter what she did, her parents were never satisfied, and they never would be.

"Do you want me to apologize?" Alanna continued. "Fine. I'll apologize. I'm sorry I didn't show up at your charity event to play the part of your perfect daughter in front of all your friends. I'm sorry I ruined your night. I'm sorry I embarrassed you by not being there. I'm sorry that I've never been anything but a disappointment to you. Is that what you're looking for?" Her voice had begun to crack with the weight of her emotion, but when she glanced up, there was no sympathy in her mother's expression. Instead Mrs. Feldman's deep brown eyes seemed darker and angrier than Alanna had ever seen them before.

Mrs. Feldman shook her head. "This is what I'm talking about, Alanna—this attitude of yours. You don't listen to a thing your father and I say, and you don't seem to think you have any sort of responsibility to this family whatsoever. It's gotten to the point where we don't even know what to do with you anymore."

"Then don't do anything," Alanna muttered. She dug her toes into the carpet and clenched her jaw. "I'm seventeen, and in another few months I'll be eighteen. Maybe it's time you and Dad stopped trying to control every single move I make."

"Why? So you can run around with that boyfriend of yours and drink yourself to death? I don't think so."

"Oh, come on, Mom. You don't—"

"I'm serious, Alanna. You need to straighten up and start concentrating on things that matter—like your family and your education. Then maybe you'll have a shot at getting into a decent college."

Alanna exhaled heavily and stared at the ceiling. "College. Is that all you care about? What *college* I go to?"

"Of course that's not all we care about, Alanna, but we're not about to just sit back and watch you ruin your life."

"I'm not ruining my life," Alanna snapped. "You are."

Mrs. Feldman sighed heavily. "That's enough. I won't stand here and let you speak to me this way. Your father and I talked about it this morning, and we're prepared to send you to an all-girls boarding school to finish out your senior year—one with extremely strict supervision. In fact, your father already has a call in to one of his friends at the Isabella Linton School for Girls, and we're hoping to hear back from her today. With any luck, we can get you into a program by the end of next week."

Alanna's jaw dropped. "You've got to be kidding," she gasped, but she could tell by the look on her mother's face that she wasn't. "An all-girls boarding school? Now? With, like, three months left in my senior year?"

"I told you, Alanna. Last night was the last straw. Your father and I don't know what else to do with you."

"But . . . you can't," Alanna protested.

"The way I see it, we don't have any other choice," Mrs. Feldman said, and before Alanna could respond, she turned on her heel and left the room.

Alanna stared after her mother, barely able to breathe. They were really planning to send her away. And with the connections that her parents had, getting her into a superstrict boarding school this late in the year would be no problem whatsoever. She fell back onto her pillow, absolutely stunned.

How did this happen? How did my life get to this point? she wondered. And how was she going to get through three months of boarding-school prison? Of course the worst part of it was that it would be three months without Conner—the only stable person in her life.

Alanna blinked rapidly, trying to stop the tears that were forming in the corners of her eyes. She couldn't do it. There was no way. If she had to go to boarding school, there was absolutely no way she was going to make it. Which meant she had to figure out how to avoid it—how to take control of her life before her parents did it for her.

*   *   *

The sound of the phone ringing was almost too much for Melissa to bear. It was as if the ringing were coming from somewhere *inside* her head instead of across the room. Reluctantly she threw back the covers, rolled out of bed, and stumbled toward the phone. There was no way she could tolerate four more rings, which was what it would take for the answering machine to pick up at this point. And since her parents always managed to answer before the second ring, it was obvious they weren't home to get it.

Besides, Melissa thought, *if it's one of my pathetic friends finally deciding to care for a minute, I want to hear it.*

"Hello?" she mumbled, realizing that not only did the room seem to be swaying, but her mouth was dry and pasty. She ran her tongue across her teeth and made a mental note to brush them as soon as she was done on the phone.

"Hello. Could I please speak to Mrs. Fox?"

Melissa groaned. She'd actually hauled herself out of bed, hangover and all, for a telemarketer. "She's not in," Melissa practically snarled.

"Oh. Well, are you authorized to make decisions regarding your long-distance calling plan?" the overly rehearsed voice inquired.

"Hardly," Melissa said. She slammed down the receiver and instantly regretted it. Even the relatively quiet sound of plastic hitting plastic seemed to echo inside her skull. *How much did I have to drink last night anyway?* she wondered as she crept across the room and crawled back into her bed. Slowly she laid her head against the pillow, lying on her side with her knees pulled up. She was hoping that if she could just lie still, the pounding in her head and the nauseating feeling in her stomach would go away. But when memories of the previous night began flashing through her head, she only felt worse.

I must have looked like such an idiot, she thought, remembering how she'd shown up to the dance drunk with Kel. Sure, Kel was a cute college guy, and everyone had been impressed at first, but Melissa was pretty sure they'd gone from impressed to repulsed sometime between Kel practically groping her on the dance floor and her yelling hysterically at Will in front of everybody.

And then she'd left the dance with Kel. Alone. Melissa pulled the covers up over her head and curled into an even tighter ball. *But what else was I supposed to do?* she thought. After the scene she'd caused, she couldn't exactly have stayed. Still, walking into a dark parking lot with a guy whose intentions were sketchy at best was one of the stupidest things she'd ever done. Yet her friends had just let her go. What were they thinking? *Couldn't they see how upset I was? How out of it I was?*

The phone started to ring again, but this time instead of jumping up to answer it, Melissa pulled her pillow over her head, determined to let the machine pick up. *If it's Gina or Cherie, I'll grab it,* she told herself. *Or Amy. Or Lila,* she added. Finally she heard her mother's too-perky voice on the announcement and then the beep. Melissa sucked in her breath and lifted the pillow so she could hear better, but it was quiet. And then there was a dial tone.

She let the pillow fall back onto her head and closed her eyes tight. *What a loser,* she chastised herself. Did she really expect anyone to call? Wasn't it obvious? No one cared. They didn't care what happened to her last night, and they obviously didn't care this morning either. The only person who'd been concerned enough to follow her out of the dance had been Jessica Wakefield. How pathetic was that? She'd been saved from eminent disaster with Kel by the one person she hated most in life. Where were her friends?

Then again, if Jessica was the only person who was even slightly worried about me last night, maybe I don't have any friends. At least not any real ones.

I should get up, Ken thought, squinting at the sunlight streaming through the crack in his shades. He glanced at his alarm clock. Ten A.M. Another half hour of sleep wouldn't hurt.

9

He rolled over and pulled his navy blue comforter up around his ears. He was just about to drift back to sleep when there was a knock at his bedroom door.

"Ken?" his father called tentatively.

For a moment Ken thought about ignoring him. Ever since he'd given up the U. Mich. football scholarship, things had been so strained between the two of them that every conversation was about as pleasurable as having a cavity filled without the benefit of novocaine.

"Ken? Are you awake?" Mr. Matthews called again. Ken sighed. He was almost eighteen. A few more months and he'd be out of his dad's house for good. It seemed like maybe he should be past the point of pretending to be asleep when his father wanted to talk to him.

"Yeah. Come on in," he answered. As his father pushed open the door, Ken sat up and leaned against the headboard of his bed. "What's up?"

Mr. Matthews cleared his throat and gazed around the room. "Nothing, really. I just thought . . ." His eyes settled on a trophy Ken had gotten as MVP of the football team his junior year. "I remember when you got this," Mr. Matthews said, picking it up and running his finger along the small plaque where Ken's name was engraved.

For a moment Mr. Matthews seemed lost in thought. But just as Ken was about to jar him back to reality by asking him what he wanted, he replaced the trophy on its shelf.

"Anyway," he said, turning to face Ken. "I just realized that my schedule's pretty clear tomorrow, and I thought it might be a good idea if we visited some of the schools you've applied to—the ones that are nearby."

Ken's eyebrows shot up. *Visit colleges? Together?* Was his father actually taking an interest in his future—even though it no longer involved football?

"If you want to, I mean," Mr. Matthews added quickly. "I just thought that since you'll probably be hearing back from some of them pretty soon, it might be wise to take a closer look at the ones within driving distance so you can start figuring out whether there's one around here you might want to attend."

Ken barely knew what to say. Had his father seriously come up with this idea on his own? "Oh. Well . . . yeah. Sure," Ken finally managed. "That would be good."

"Okay," Mr. Matthews said with a nod. He stood silently gazing around the room for another minute—just long enough for the silence between them to begin to feel awkward—then nodded again. "All right, then. Tomorrow," he said, stepping out and closing the door behind him.

Ken stared at the white wooden door and frowned. *What was that about?* he wondered. Did his father honestly care where he went now that football wasn't a factor? It didn't seem likely. *Maybe Mom called and asked him to take me,* Ken thought. Although judging by how infrequently his father had taken his mother's advice in the past, he didn't think that was probable either. But it wasn't as if Mr. Matthews could have gotten the idea from a girlfriend who was trying to make a good impression on his son—he wasn't seeing anyone at the moment. So maybe he really had come up with it on his own.

Ken took a deep breath and decided he shouldn't question it. After all, if his father was honestly making an effort to support his going to school for academics instead of football, it didn't really matter where the idea to visit a few schools had come from. All that mattered was that his father was trying. And the least Ken could do was accept it.

Will tipped back his glass of orange juice and downed the last third of it in one gulp. He'd slept in way too late. It was eleven-thirty already, and he was just having breakfast. At least he knew he could call

Erika now without waking her up—not that he actually cared. After the way she'd disappeared at the dance last night, leaving him on his own, she deserved to be jolted out of bed by the phone.

He walked into the hallway and grabbed the cordless phone, then went up to his room, where he dialed Erika's number. It took five rings, but finally she picked up. Clumsily. From Will's end, it sounded as though she had banged the receiver against every conceivable object between its cradle and her ear.

"Hello?" she said in a raspy voice.

Good, Will thought smugly. *I did wake her.* Of course, he wasn't about to apologize. "Hey. It's Will," he said coolly. *You know, the guy you supposedly had a date with last night?*

"Oh, hi. Hey—what time is it anyway?" she asked. It sounded like she was closer to falling asleep again than actually waking up.

"Eleven-thirty. Why?"

"Oh, wow. I don't usually sleep this late—I must be exhausted. Then again, I didn't get in until two this morning."

"Two?" Will echoed. Obviously Erika hadn't gone straight home after leaving him.

"Yeah," she said with a giggle. "I went out with a couple of old friends I met up with at the dance—which was a blast, by the way. Thanks for taking me."

Will's jaw dropped. The girl had *ditched* him, and she didn't even seem to get that he might be slightly upset about it. "Yeah. Sure," he muttered.

"It really was great to see some of my old friends."

"I bet," Will said.

"Oh—and did you realize that Paul Davis went to El Carro?"

Will squinted. "You mean *Coach* Davis?" he asked.

Again Erika giggled. "That's so cute. Do you really call him 'Coach'?"

The way Erika said *cute* made Will's stomach turn. "Well, he is the assistant coach for the girls' basketball team," he retorted.

"I know," Erika said. "But anyway, he was a senior at El Carro when I was a freshman, and I had the biggest crush on him." Great. Now she was talking about other guys. What was wrong with this girl? *More like what's wrong with me,* Will thought. He was beginning to realize that Erika had never intended to be his girlfriend—at least not in the way he had imagined. In fact, it was beginning to sound like she'd never even meant to be his date. More like a flirty friend along for the ride.

"So I told him all about it last night," Erika continued.

"Wait," Will interrupted. "You told who what?"

"Paul. You know—*Coach Davis,*" she added in

14

what Will took to be a condescending tone. "I told him that I had a major crush on him when I was a freshman, then one thing led to another, and he asked me out. So I'm getting together with him tonight to talk about old times—you know, before the earthquake."

And before I was dumb enough to fall for a college girl, Will thought. What an idiot. Erika was hot, all right, but she seemed to think it was fine to go to a dance with him, leave with someone else, and then date someone completely new the next night. *Definitely not my style,* Will told himself.

"Will? Are you still there?"

"Huh? Oh, yeah," Will said, although whatever Erika had been saying, he'd missed it.

"So anyway, I'm glad that you're okay with it."

"With what?"

"With me going out with Paul tonight," Erika explained.

"Oh. Yeah. Whatever," Will said.

"Because you know, sometimes guys—especially high-school guys—expect a girl to date them exclusively right from the start. But I like to keep my options open."

"Yeah. Me too," Will lied.

"Cool. So maybe we can go out again sometime."

"Sure," Will said, although he had no intention of

following up on it. He still couldn't believe he'd been so stupid as to think that he'd actually had a shot with her. But at least he had one consolation. Erika's rotation in the sports department at the *Tribune* would be coming to an end soon, and then he wouldn't have to work with her anymore. He wouldn't even have to see her, and that was just fine with him.

Alanna Feldman

<u>Options:</u>

Wait a day and try to talk this out with Mom and Dad when they've had some time to cool off.

Get out of here faster than Superman racing a speeding bullet.

All right. First, if I wait a day to do anything, it may be too late. The way my mother was talking this morning, she's planning to ship me off ASAP. So in twenty-four hours I could be on my way to The Citadel. They take girls now, right?

Second, I've never been able to talk <u>anything</u> out with my parents. Not what clothes I can wear, which friends I can hang out with, what guys I can date. Nothing. So I doubt they're going to pour me a cup of tea and ask me to sit down and share my thoughts about boarding school. Which means I'm left with option number two.

But where am I going to go? And how will I get there?

Okay. I guess I do have one other option.

Call Conner.

He's always been able to help me before. And besides, if I leave, maybe he can come with me. At least part of the way.

CHAPTER 2
No More Trouble

Conner will know what to do, Alanna thought. *He always does.*

She paced the floor of her room, gripping the phone a little tighter with each unanswered ring. *Please be home. Please be—*

"Hello?"

"Conner!"

"Alanna. I was just about to call you."

In spite of everything that was going on, Alanna smiled. It was so good to hear his voice—his calm, rational, perpetually sexy voice. "You were?" she asked.

"Yeah, I've got news."

Me too, Alanna thought, although she could tell from Conner's uncharacteristically chipper voice that his news was much better.

"You know that school with the incredible music program?" he asked. "The one I sent all those writing samples and audition tapes to?"

"Yeah," Alanna answered. How could she forget?

19

It was practically the only place Conner had any interest in going to. He'd even said that if he didn't get in, he might just take a year off and try to travel or something, which to Alanna had sounded pretty good. Especially now that she was planning to do a little traveling herself.

"Well, they called this morning," Conner continued. "They invited me to their West Coast auditions on Wednesday."

"Conner, that's great," Alanna said. "Congratulations." At least someone was having a good day.

"Yeah, it should be cool," he replied. "I guess it's going to be part interview, part audition. I'm supposed to bring my guitar and be ready to play a few songs or something."

Again Alanna was struck by how upbeat Conner sounded. Normally he was so mellow, so reserved. "That's fantastic," she said, trying to affect an encouraging tone. She didn't want to bring him down by shifting his focus onto her problems.

"Yeah," he agreed.

There was a brief silence, during which Alanna tried to think of a subtle way to get some advice from Conner without actually telling him what was going on. But there didn't seem to be anything she could say without arousing suspicion—he knew her too well. *And he's saved me too many times,* Alanna thought.

"So what's up with you?" Conner asked.

Alanna hesitated. As much as she wanted to pour out all the details and tell him what a mess her life was, she knew she couldn't. Not now. Not when he was so excited about his future and the incredible opportunity he was being given.

"Not much," she lied. "I just wanted to say hi. And thank you for taking me to the dance last night. I know you don't usually go to those kinds of things, but I had a really good time."

"No problem," Conner said, reverting to his normal, less-than-chatty self. Again there was a silence, and Alanna knew that she had to get off the phone quickly.

"Well, I should probably let you go," she said, trying to keep the emotion out of her voice. Already her eyes were beginning to water. She couldn't help thinking that this might be the last chance she had to talk to him, and the thought of leaving him behind— actually letting him go—was almost too much to take.

"All right," Conner said. "I'll talk to you later."

Much later, Alanna thought. If at all. But she resisted saying anything to Conner. For once things seemed to be falling into place for him, and there was no way she was going to bring him down with the details of her pathetic life. This was one crisis she was going to have to handle on her own.

Alanna Feldman

http://www.u-travel.com/reservations.html

Thank you for using U-Travel.com. Your airline ticket will be held for you at the designated airline counter. Your confirmation number for this transaction is 01G3672F7IBM3. Please make a note of it.

Did you know we can also arrange your transportation to and from the airport? Click <u>here</u> for details.

Wow. So that's it. My flight's booked. Is there anything you <u>can't</u> do online? Probably not, but the strangest part is that I wouldn't even be able to do this if my parents hadn't set me up with my own credit card.

It was one of those "just in case of emergency" things: You know, like the way some parents give their kids a few extra dollars to carry around or a prepaid calling card or something. Of course, my parents had to go one better than everyone else. So I got the calling card and the cash, and when I turned sixteen, they got me this card. With a twenty-thousand-dollar limit. Sometimes I don't know what they're thinking—not that I'm complaining.

I've had it for almost two years now, and I've never used it. And truthfully, I think my parents have forgotten all about it. They must have. Otherwise they would have taken it away by now.

So then I guess they're going to be pretty freaked out when they realize the emergency I finally used it for was to get away from them.

Will stared blankly at the Web page in front of him. It was dedicated completely to animal crackers. The history of animal crackers, comparisons of different brands, various methods for eating them, debates over dunking versus eating them dry.

"I can't believe this," he muttered, clicking numbly through the pages.

For the past two hours—ever since he'd gotten off the phone with Erika—he'd been sitting in front of the computer, randomly entering URLs just to see what was out there. And also to keep his mind off Erika and what an idiot he'd been to think they'd actually had something between them. It seemed as though there wasn't anything left in the world without its own Web site. Although there wasn't one dedicated to Erika Brooks. Will had checked.

He was just about to type in www.useless.com when the phone rang. Will glared at it. If it hadn't been sitting on the desk right next to him, he would have ignored it. He didn't feel like talking to anyone, but he couldn't quite rationalize just letting it ring when the phone was practically in his hand.

Reluctantly he picked up the receiver and pressed talk. "Hello?"

"Hey, Will. It's Josh."

"Oh. Hi."

"What's up, man? How did the rest of your date with Erika go last night? I didn't see the two of you after the dance. Does that mean you left early?" Will grimaced. He could practically see the goofy grin on Josh's face—the one that meant he was anticipating some juicy details. Too bad Will didn't have any.

"Yeah, I guess we did head out before it was over," Will said, which was true. More or less. It wasn't his fault if Josh assumed he meant *together*.

"Where to?"

"What do you mean?"

"*Well* . . . did you go somewhere else, like for coffee or something, or did you just go home?"

Will hesitated. That question was going to be a little more difficult to dodge. "Uh . . . we pretty much just went home," he said.

"Really?" Josh asked, his disappointment evident in his tone.

"I mean, you know, we talked for a while and stuff," Will added, hoping Josh would interpret *stuff* liberally.

"Yeah? And how was that?" Josh asked. His goofy grin was obviously back in place.

"It was okay."

"*Okay?*"

"Yeah. I mean, Erika's hot and everything, but after a while that gets kind of . . . boring, you know?"

"*Boring?*" Josh echoed. "You're kidding, right?"

"No, I'm serious. I mean, *hot* only goes so far. Something else has to be there eventually, right?"

Josh snorted. "I don't know. I think I could get by with *hot* and nothing else for a long time."

"Yeah, well . . ."

"This doesn't have anything to do with Melissa and her little scene, does it?" Josh asked.

Melissa. Will closed his eyes. He'd almost forgotten how trashed she was last night. "Uh, no. Not really." How had she gotten home anyway? "Hey— did you see her last night? I mean after the dance?"

"No. She left with that college guy, remember? Right after she finished bitching you out, the two of them walked out arm in arm. Although it was more like her body in his arms from where I was standing. I don't think she could have made it on her own."

Oh, crap, Will thought. *She shouldn't have left with that guy. I shouldn't have let her.* Sure, he'd been pretty wrapped up in Erika, but even so, he could still tell that Kim or Kyle—whatever his name was—was a jerk.

"Will? You still there?"

"Oh, yeah. Sorry. I guess I just zoned out."

"Yeah, well, a date with Erika Brooks will do that to you."

Will forced a laugh.

"So anyway, I'll talk to you later," Josh said. "And Will?"

"Yeah?"

"If you decide not to go out with Erika again, could you at least give her my number first?"

"Sure thing," Will said. "Talk to you later."

Will pressed the off button, but he didn't set down the phone. He couldn't get the image of Melissa yelling at him in front of everybody out of his head. Or the image of that creep with his hands all over her every time they'd danced. If she'd really been stupid enough to leave with him, she could be in big trouble right now.

Without another thought, Will punched in Melissa's number and waited anxiously through six rings. The machine picked up, but at the same time some-one else did as well.

"Hello?" Mrs. Fox said over the sound of her own voice on the announcement. "Oh, hold on a second." There was the muffled sound of her fidgeting with something, and then the recording stopped. "There. Sorry about that. I just got in from the store."

"That's okay, uh, Mrs. Fox?" Will said, even though he knew it was her.

"Yes. Will?"

"Yeah."

"It's good to hear from you. How are things going?"

"Pretty good, thanks," Will managed, even though he wasn't in the mood for their usual round of small talk. "Hey, I was wondering if Melissa was around," he said.

"I'm sure she is. Let me go get her for you. Nice talking to you, Will."

"You too, Mrs. Fox," Will said. He knew Melissa's mother liked him a lot, but the feeling wasn't mutual. In all the time he'd known Melissa, he'd never seen her mother do anything but hurt her. Still, it helped to have an ally in the family, and he wasn't about to jeopardize that.

"Will?" It was Mrs. Fox again.

"Yeah?"

"I'm sorry. Melissa is . . ." Mrs. Fox exhaled heavily, and Will could tell she was angry. She always sighed like that when she felt put out by something or someone—usually Melissa. "She's not able to come to the phone right now."

"Oh, uh . . . okay."

"Maybe you could try again later," Mrs. Fox suggested.

"Yeah, sure," Will said, but he already knew he wasn't going to be calling back.

Not able to come to the phone, huh? Where did she get off anyway? Here he was calling her out of concern, and she refused to even talk to him.

That's it, Will told himself. He was through with Melissa and her head games. If she wanted to get trashed and go home with college guys, let her. He wasn't going to waste any more of his time looking out for her. Let Kevin or Kirk deal with her moody games. He was finished.

"Aren't you kind of young to be traveling alone at this time of night?" Bert asked. Bert was the taxi driver who had picked Alanna up to go to the airport. He'd introduced himself the minute she got in, and he'd been making conversation with her ever since. He eyed her in the rearview mirror. "You can't be more than eighteen," he said. "I've got a daughter about your age."

Alanna raised her eyebrows. From his abundance of white hair and the wrinkles around his eyes she would have guessed he had a *granddaughter* her age, but she didn't say so.

"Courtney's her name. She's my youngest. My baby. Bullheaded as they come, but she's a sweetheart underneath. She's grown up way too fast."

"Yeah, my parents say the same thing," Alanna said, though she was pretty sure they'd never said anything quite so nice to her. If anything, they probably wished she'd grow up faster so she wouldn't be their problem anymore.

"It's true, you know," Bert said. "One minute you're a baby, the next minute you're getting ready to graduate from high school."

"Oh, well, actually, I'm twenty," Alanna told him, trying to sound confident. "But I know what you mean."

"Twenty?" His eyes flicked to the mirror again, sizing her up. "Still a bit young to be headed to the airport at this hour, isn't it?"

Alanna sighed. So they were back to this again. How much farther could the airport be?

"Not really," she said. "I've been home from college, and now I'm headed back. It's always cheaper to fly at night." She had no idea if that was actually true, and in reality her flight didn't leave until 6 A.M., but she hoped it would satisfy Bert. All his questions were beginning to make her feel like a fugitive, and she didn't need any help with that. Leaving home was unsettling enough without Santa Claus up there playing twenty questions.

"Is it now?" he asked. "Well, I suppose that makes sense. Who wants to deal with airlines at this hour?"

Alanna forced a slight chuckle. *Gee, I don't know,* she thought. *Teenagers running away from home, maybe?* She wondered what Bert would do if he knew the truth—that she had sneaked downstairs after she was sure her parents were asleep, raided her father's secret stash of money in the top drawer of his desk, and crept out without leaving so much as a note. He'd probably pull over and try to talk some sense into her. He seemed like a decent dad. Surely

30

his daughter—Courtney, bullheaded as she might be—would never pull such a stunt.

Finally Alanna saw a sign for the airport and relaxed her shoulders slightly. The exit was only a mile away. In less than five minutes she'd be at the terminal, and she wouldn't have to answer any more of Bert's questions. Hopefully none of the people at the airline counter would be quite so chatty. Then she could just get her ticket and be on her way.

"So where's your school?" Bert asked.

"My school?"

"Yes. Your college. Where are you headed?"

"Oh," Alanna breathed, thankful that Bert had clarified his question. She'd been on the verge of telling him the actual name of her high school. "Uh, Florida. The University of Florida at Miami," she pulled from out of nowhere. There was no sense in telling him where she was really headed. Why be truthful now? She was on a roll.

"Ah. Miami. Nice place," Bert said, and thankfully he didn't ask her any questions about the school or its campus. She'd never even seen so much as a brochure. *Next time,* she told herself, *pick a place you know.*

Bert took the airport exit without a word—apparently getting through the maze of an entrance took a little bit of concentration. When he finally pulled up at her terminal, Alanna breathed a sigh of

31

relief. She'd survived her first test—lying through her teeth to one of the nicest men she'd met in ages.

She stepped out of the cab, and Bert got out too, to retrieve her duffel bag from the trunk. "Well, good luck at school," he said, handing the bag to her as she fumbled for a twenty and some ones to cover the fare.

"Thanks," Alanna said, aware that her voice was a bit shaky. Somehow the fact that she was actually leaving hadn't hit her until that very moment. Any second now Bert was going to pull away in his cab, and she was going to be all alone. She watched as he opened the driver's-side door and started to get in, but then he stopped.

"Forgive me for being nosy," he said, "but I have one more question." Alanna stared at him, frozen. "If you were home visiting, why did you have me pick you up at a convenience store instead of your house?"

Alanna swallowed hard. He was nice and obviously a protective, fatherly type. Part of her wanted to tell him the truth, but she couldn't risk it. If she ended up back at her parents' house after trying to run away, they'd have her on the first bus to St. Whoever's-it-was and probably in a straitjacket too.

"Oh, well, that's the problem with traveling so late. I have a couple of younger sisters, and I didn't want to wake them up stumbling out with all my stuff at midnight. So I said good-bye after dinner, grabbed some coffee with a friend, and had her drop me at the store so I could pick up a few magazines for the flight." Bert eyed her doubtfully, and Alanna forced herself to hold his gaze. "That's the way I always do it," she added with a shrug.

Bert nodded. "Well . . . good luck," he said, getting into his cab. He'd either bought her story or decided it was really none of his business, Alanna wasn't sure which. And it didn't matter. Because once the cab pulled away, she knew she would probably never see him again. In fact, there were a lot of people she was probably never going to see again. Like Conner, for instance. The only one who mattered.

Melissa Fox

To: <u>cherier@swiftnet.com</u>,
<u>gina22@swiftnet.com</u>, <u>lila@fowler.com</u>,
<u>amysutton13@swiftnet.com</u>
From: <u>mfox@swiftnet.com</u>
Subject: Friends?

I can't believe the way you guys deserted me. First, inviting Will and Erika to hang out with you and your sad excuses for dates when you know how much I hate her and then just watching me leave with Kel when you all must have known how out of it I was. You call yourselves friends? Well, I guess I know the truth now, and as far as I'm concerned, you can forget about ever being my friends again. Let's just see how far you get without me. I'm the one who made you all popular, you know, so don't be surprised if all the guys stop calling once I'm gone.

<Delete message>

To: wsimmons@swiftnet.com
From: mfox@swiftnet.com
Subject: Jerk

My mother said you called this afternoon. Why? To tell me all about your date with Erika? Seriously, why did you bother? Did you honestly think I would talk to you after everything that's happened? Get a clue. Besides, I don't date high-school guys anymore. They're all like you—way too immature.

<Delete message>

Forget this. I can't think straight, and my eyes still hurt way too much to be staring at a computer screen. I'm going back to bed.

CHAPTER

Why Bother?

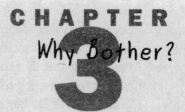

3

Conner plucked at his guitar strings, switching rapidly from a G7 chord to A and back again. "That's it," he said quietly. After the loop he needed to go to A—not C.

The piece he was working on was purely instrumental at this point, and it seemed okay that way. For once Conner didn't feel compelled to add lyrics. Gavin, his guitar instructor, had said it was his "most complex," the song that "best demonstrated his talent as a musician," and Conner was hoping the people at his audition would agree.

He glanced at the clock on his nightstand, stunned to see that it was already two. He'd been practicing for three hours now. He was actually spending a Sunday afternoon *working* on something. Working *toward* something—willingly. For once things seemed to be falling into place for him.

He was just about to play through the newly changed part of his song again to make sure he had it down when there was a knock at the door.

"Conner," his sister Megan called. "Phone."

"Take a message," he called back.

"Too late. I already said you were here," Megan replied, her voice trailing off down the hallway.

Conner sighed. He hated being interrupted when he was in a groove. Reluctantly he leaned his guitar against his bed and walked out to the hallway, where Megan had left the receiver sitting on the phone table.

"Hello?"

"Where is my daughter?" an angry voice barked.

"What?"

"You heard me," the woman continued. "I want to know where Alanna is, and I want to know this instant. I know she's with you."

Conner rolled his eyes. Mrs. Feldman had definitely gone off the deep end this time. "I don't know where she is," he said. "I haven't even talked with her since yesterday morning. And I haven't seen her since Friday night."

"Oh, yes, Friday night. Thanks for reminding me," Mrs. Feldman replied. "How dare you convince my daughter to skip a family function for a ridiculous dance? Don't you understand the meaning of the word *responsibility?*"

"What?" Conner said. The woman was clearly losing it.

"You know perfectly well what I'm talking about,"

38

Mrs. Feldman sneered. "Don't play innocent with me. I want my daughter home by dinnertime, or I'm calling the police."

"I told you—she's *not here*," he snapped, but Mrs. Feldman had already hung up. Conner looked at the receiver and shook his head before setting it down.

"What was that about?" his mother asked. She was just coming up the stairs with an armful of clean towels, and she must have caught the last part of the conversation.

"Nothing," Conner said. "Just Mrs. Feldman sending her best."

Mrs. Sandborn pressed her lips together—suppressing a smile, Conner thought. "Is everything all right with Alanna?" she asked.

"Yeah. Probably."

"Probably?"

Conner shrugged. "Well, she's not at home and her mom doesn't know where she is, but that's not exactly surprising."

Mrs. Sandborn tilted her head. "No, I suppose not," she said, opening the linen closet and piling the towels onto their shelves. "It's much harder to keep track of a child who's almost eighteen than it is to keep track of a younger one."

Conner scowled, knowing the comment was aimed at him.

"Do you really think she's okay?" Mrs. Sandborn asked.

"Yeah," he said after a moment, deciding it would be better if he didn't mention Mrs. Feldman's threat about calling the police. "She probably just went for a walk. I know I wouldn't want to be stuck inside with her parents all day." Mrs. Sandborn nodded and headed back down the stairs. Conner turned and shuffled into his room, closing the door behind him.

He picked up his guitar and tried to get back into the frame of mind he'd been in before the phone call, but it was useless. All he kept thinking about was Alanna and where she might be. It didn't surprise him that Mrs. Feldman had no clue where she was. Alanna didn't exactly confide in her parents about the details of her life.

Conner strummed a few chords and thought, clenching and unclenching his jaw. Alanna had sounded a little weird on the phone yesterday, and she'd gotten off kind of quickly after he'd told her about his audition. But that was probably just because of the whole going-away-to-college thing, the idea that they'd be headed in different directions in the fall. At least that was what he'd figured—until her mom had called.

Mrs. Feldman had seemed so freaked out—not like her usual ranting self. This time she'd sounded desperate.

Conner shook his head. He shouldn't let it get to him. For one thing, he couldn't imagine that Mrs. Feldman had even a single ounce of maternal instinct in her body. She was probably flipping because Alanna was going to miss another "family function." And second, it wasn't like this was the first time Alanna had gone out without telling her parents.

Still, there was one thing he couldn't quite figure out. Where would she have gone without telling *him?*

"And here we are back at the library," the student tour guide said, nodding toward the large brick building before them. "Do you have any questions?"

The three other sets of parents and kids in their group shook their heads, and Ken was about to say "no" and "thank you" as well, but his father jumped right in. "Are you familiar with the football program here?" Mr. Matthews asked. Ken rolled his eyes. From the tour guide's jet-black hair, eyeliner, and clothing—not to mention the silver stud in her nose—he suspected she was more likely to attend poetry readings than football games. But of course, to his father, everything revolved around sports, and it would be unthinkable that anyone—including this girl—could attend a college without being familiar with its football program.

"I wouldn't call it my strong point," she said, "but what in particular did you want to know about it?"

"Well, my son probably has a good shot at making the team—if I can convince him to try out," Mr. Matthews said with a grin. The way he was playing up his fatherly role made Ken's stomach lurch. All of a sudden he was acting like some kind of TV dad, from an old show like *The Brady Bunch,* where the family was superclose and every episode ended with a group hug.

"Great," said the tour guide, nodding at Ken with the phoniest smile he'd ever seen. She was probably composing a haiku about dumb jocks in her head.

"Now, I know that UCLA has pretty strict GPA requirements for its students, so I guess I'm wondering if those standards might be a little less stringent for students involved in serious athletic endeavors."

Ken's jaw dropped. He glanced around at the other parents who were still within hearing distance and saw more than one of them turn to glare at his father with a disapproving frown.

"Ah," said the tour guide, stealing a look at Ken. "Well, as far as I know, student athletes are held to the same standards as everyone else," she said slowly, and Ken felt his cheeks beginning to burn. How could his father have asked such a stupid question? Sure, Ken's grades weren't the best—he knew that. He hadn't even wanted to apply to UCLA in the first place, but Mr. Nelson had convinced him to, arguing that with the improvements he'd made during his senior year, he actually stood a chance. And for a while Ken had actually started to believe him—at least he hadn't received a rejection letter yet, and those usually came early.

But then along came his father, knocking him back into reality once again. Not to mention demonstrating the level of confidence he had in his son's ability to get by without extra help.

"Well, I guess that's something we can talk about with the athletic director," Mr. Matthews said, nodding toward Ken as if it were a concern they shared.

"Yeah. I guess you can," said the tour guide. She glanced toward Ken again, and this time he got the distinct impression that her eyes were narrowed at him more in pity than contempt.

That's right, he thought, glaring back at her. *I'm a dumb jock. And the only way I'm ever going to show up at one of your coffeehouses is if the football coach gets the English professor to offer me extra credit for it.*

She raised her eyebrows and looked away. "Well, if there aren't any other questions," she said hopefully.

"Not from me," Mr. Matthews said, and it struck Ken that he didn't seem the least bit embarrassed about anything he'd said. Then again, after bribing a football scout to get his son into one college, asking flat out for special consideration at another one probably seemed downright noble. "Ken?" he asked.

"No," Ken mumbled, refusing to meet his father's eyes. Although he did have one question that kept kicking around inside his head. *Why do I even bother?*

"May I have your attention, please," a muffled voice called over the loudspeaker. "Blah-blah-blah Airlines is pleased to announce it is now boarding flight eighty-blah twenty-two, nonstop service to blah. Passengers in rows thirty-blah through forty-five may now begin boarding at gate blah."

It seemed to Alanna that all of the important words were blurred every time an announcement was made—not that she cared. She'd reached her destination. Now all she had to do was find a phone and call Lisa.

Lisa Bresinsky had been her best friend up until sophomore year, when Mrs. Bresinsky had gotten a new job teaching at the University of Chicago and moved the whole family there. Of course, Alanna and Lisa had kept in touch with occasional letters and e-mails for a while, but their correspondence had dropped off over the last six months or so—about the same time period during which Alanna's alcohol consumption had seriously picked up.

Still, Alanna was pretty sure Lisa would help her out. They'd been friends since second grade, and several times when they were thirteen and fourteen, Lisa had covered for Alanna by saying they were going to the movies together when Alanna was actually meeting up with one boyfriend or another. Besides, yesterday, when Alanna had realized once and for all that she needed to get out of town before her parents shipped her off to a convent, she hadn't been able to think of anyone else to turn to. Except Conner, of course. But she was through messing up his life.

She made her way past the baggage carousel across a beautiful granite or marble floor—she didn't really know which, only that it seemed wasted in an airport—to a bank of phones that lined one wall. She stepped up to one of the phones, dropped her duffel on the floor, and reached into the back pocket of her jeans to pull out the scrap of paper with Lisa's number.

After punching in an endless succession of numbers—first her calling-card number, then her PIN, then Lisa's phone number—Alanna finally heard a ringing tone, and her hand started to shake. What if the number was wrong? What if one of Lisa's parents answered? What if Lisa was angry that Alanna had stopped writing and decided not to help? Then someone answered.

"Hello?"

Alanna let out a sigh of relief at the sound of her friend's voice. "Hi, Lisa, this is Alanna. I'm really sorry to bother you, but—"

"Hey—how are you?"

"Uh . . . *okay*," Alanna answered.

"Have you been running?" Lisa asked. "You sound like you're out of breath."

Running? Only away, Alanna thought. Of course, the reason she sounded out of breath was that she had been holding hers ever since she'd punched the last number.

"Uh, no, not running, really, but . . . I'm kind of in some trouble."

Lisa laughed. "Really? *You?* In trouble? That's a new one," she teased. If Lisa had been aware of half the stuff Alanna had been through in the last six months, she would have felt horrible for making such a comment, but she obviously didn't have a clue. And how would she? Alanna hadn't exactly been keeping her informed.

"Yeah, well, this time it's a little more serious," Alanna said.

"Really? Why? What's up?" Lisa asked. Suddenly her voice had gotten quieter.

"Are you alone?"

"No, but I will be," Lisa said in a chipper tone that was obviously meant to be overheard. "Can you hold on a minute?"

"Sure."

"It's Kelly," Alanna heard her say to whoever else was with her. "What time will you guys be home?"

46

Alanna couldn't make out what the other voices were saying, only that there were at least two of them, most likely Lisa's parents. "I'll probably be in bed. No, I might catch a movie or something, but if I do, I'll leave a note. Okay. Bye."

There was a pause, then Alanna heard a door slam. "Sorry," Lisa said, her voice back to its regular volume. "That was my parents. They just left."

"Well, I'm glad you didn't tell them it was me on the phone," Alanna said.

"Something told me not to," Lisa said. "So what's going on? What kind of trouble are you in?"

"Well . . ." Alanna wasn't quite sure where to start. "For one thing, I'm in Chicago."

"That's great!" Lisa said. "Why? Does your dad have a conference or something?"

"Not exactly . . ."

"Well, then—what for?"

"To see you," Alanna said, figuring that was a good place to start. She couldn't exactly jump into all the details over the phone anyway.

"Really?" Lisa asked. "I mean, that's totally cool, but isn't it kind of risky to travel so far for a surprise visit?"

Alanna didn't answer. There was a silence at the other end, and she almost thought she could hear the pieces clicking into place inside Lisa's brain.

47

"Oh my God," Lisa said finally. "Do your parents know you're here?"

"No. And they can't find out," Alanna told her.

"*Alanna*—oh my God! What are you doing? You can't just take off across the country without telling your parents."

"Look, I know it doesn't sound good, but I *had* to—believe me. They were going to send me to some kind of reform school for wayward girls or something. I had to get away."

"They wouldn't do that," Lisa said.

"Are you serious? Have you forgotten what my parents are like? They absolutely would, and they were going to if I stayed there one more minute," Alanna insisted.

"But do you really think running away is the answer?"

"For right now I do," Alanna said. "I just need some time to think, some time to figure things out, and they weren't going to give me that. They wanted to ship me off so they wouldn't have to deal with me anymore."

"I'm sure that's not true. They're your *parents*, Alanna. They love you."

"They may be my parents, and they might even think they love me, but that doesn't mean they know what's right for me, and I'm not about to spend three months in prison just to make things easier for them."

Lisa sighed, and Alanna knew she was beginning to break down. "So—why are you calling me? What do you want me to do?" Lisa asked. It was the opening Alanna had been waiting for.

"I need a place to stay—just for a few days while I figure out what to do next."

"Well, of course you can stay with us," Lisa replied. "I'm sure my parents would—"

"No way," Alanna interrupted. "You can't tell your parents I'm here. The first thing they'd do is get on the phone to my parents, who'd be on the next plane here—probably with a police escort."

"But how can I *not* tell my parents?" Lisa protested. "I mean, if you're staying here, they're bound to see you sooner or later."

"Not if we're careful," Alanna said.

"You've got to be kidding," Lisa replied. "Do you honestly think you can stay at my house without having my parents catch on?"

"I don't know. I've never seen your house. But if it's anywhere near as big as that mansion you lived in back in California, yeah. I think I could."

"It's not," Lisa said. Alanna waited patiently. Even when they had been kids, just eight years old, Lisa had always needed to be coaxed into everything. "Although . . ."

"*What?*" Alanna said, tightening her grip on the receiver.

"Well, there is a room over the garage that no one uses."

"Perfect," Alanna said.

"It's not perfect," Lisa disagreed. "It's my brother's room, and my mom still goes in to clean and stuff once in a while. But he's away at college right now, and he won't be home for another few weeks, so it should be safe. For a couple of days anyway."

"Oh, Lisa—thank you so much," Alanna said. "And I promise—it's only for a few days."

"Then you'll call your parents, right? Or at least let me tell mine so they can call?"

"Sure," Alanna agreed. There was no harm in telling Lisa a small lie. Especially when she knew it would make her feel better about the whole situation. "So when can I come over?"

"Well, my parents just left to do some shopping and go out to dinner, so if you can come now, they won't see you."

"Great."

"How are you going to get here?"

"I figured I'd just take a taxi—I have your address and everything."

"Yeah, but if you show up in a taxi, one of our neighbors might see, and then they'd ask Mom if Jeff was home for a visit, and pretty soon she'd know someone had shown up in a taxi and she'd want to know who."

"Seriously?"

"Yes, seriously. Our neighborhood is . . . cozy."

"More like *nosy*," Alanna said.

"Whatever," Lisa said. "So anyway, why don't I pick you up? Are you at O'Hare?"

"Yeah—where do you want to meet?"

"How about next to the cab stand just outside Terminal A—that's the easiest one to get to."

"Okay," Alanna said, glancing at all of the signs around her. She wasn't even sure which terminal she was in now, but certainly she could find A by the time Lisa arrived.

"All right. About a half hour, then," Lisa said. "And after a few days you promise you'll call your parents?"

"I promise," Alanna said, crossing her fingers behind her back as she spoke. It was childish, she knew, but it made her feel a little better about lying to her best friend. At least for now.

Will Simmons

You know, I've been thinking about it, and just because Melissa didn't come to the phone, it doesn't mean she didn't want to talk to me. What did her mom say? "Melissa isn't able to come to the phone," right? Which could just as easily have meant that she was in the shower. Or, judging by how drunk she was last night, maybe she was throwing up. That would explain why Mrs. Fox sounded so disgusted. She definitely wouldn't approve of Melissa getting wasted.

So anyway, I think I'm going to try again. Because whether Melissa wants to admit it or not—she needs me. And besides, it's not like I have anything better to do.

"You should come with us, Melissa," Mrs. Fox said. "We're going to try the new sushi bar that just opened on Middle Street."

"I don't like sushi," Melissa said with a scowl. She walked over to the refrigerator and opened it up, looking for something she could snack on and call dinner.

"Yes, you do," her mother said. "You tried some at your cousin Danny's wedding, and you loved it."

"I don't remember that," Melissa said, although vaguely she did. She just didn't want to admit it.

"Well, I do. And don't just stand there with the door open—you're wasting electricity."

"As if you care," Melissa said, shutting the refrigerator. Her mother stopped rummaging through her pocketbook long enough to fix Melissa with an icy stare.

"What is wrong with you anyway?" Mrs. Fox asked. "You wouldn't talk to Will yesterday, you stayed home last night—a *Saturday night*—for the first time

53

in years, and you're definitely in one of your less than pleasant moods today. Is something going on?"

Melissa almost laughed. Her mother was practically shouting at her. Was that her way of being nurturing? *This must be where I'm supposed to break down and cry on her shoulder,* Melissa thought.

"No. Nothing's going on. I'm fine."

Mrs. Fox narrowed her eyes. "You certainly don't seem fine."

"Well, I am. So just leave me alone, okay?" Melissa walked back to the refrigerator and opened it again, scanning its contents partly because she was genuinely hungry and partly to tick off her mother.

"Are you sure you're all right?" Mrs. Fox asked. "We could stay home and order pizza instead," she offered, but Melissa knew what she wanted to hear.

"I'm fine. Just go." Melissa felt her mother's eyes on her back, but she refused to turn around.

"All right," Mrs. Fox said finally. "But call my cell phone if you need anything, okay?"

"Sure," Melissa muttered. *Parenting by cell phone,* she mused. *Will the wonders of technology never cease?*

Mrs. Fox grabbed her pocketbook from the counter and slung it over her shoulder, then opened the kitchen door. "Roger—I'm going out to check the geraniums," she yelled to her husband. "I'll meet you at the car."

"Good riddance," Melissa muttered as her mother exited through one door and her father entered through another.

"What was that?" her father asked. He smelled like cologne, and his hair was still wet, his face freshly shaven.

"Nothing," Melissa said, inhaling his clean, soapy smell. She used to love to watch him shave when she was little. He always looked so funny with his face all lathered up, and sometimes he would kiss her on the nose, leaving a little dollop of shaving cream behind. It had never failed to make her laugh, but now they barely did anything together. It was as if somewhere along the line she'd stopped being his little girl, or at least that's how it felt.

"Your mom and I are going to dinner. We're going to try—"

"The new sushi bar. I know," Melissa said.

"Oh. Well, do you want to come?"

"No. Thanks."

"You sure?"

"*Yes, Dad*," Melissa droned. Even he was getting on her nerves tonight.

"All right. Well, we'll bring you back something," he said, obviously trying to elicit a grin or at least some kind of reaction, but Melissa didn't have it in her. She kept her eyes fixed on the half-empty milk container until she heard the door swing shut behind him.

Then, when she was sure they were gone, she closed the refrigerator and turned to lean against it. Why did they always have to go out? Not that it would be any different if they stayed home. She still wouldn't be able to talk to them. But at least she wouldn't be alone.

She walked to the kitchen window just in time to see their car pull out, and for a second she contemplated running out to stop them. It wasn't like she had to make conversation with them or anything— she could just eat. And she did like sushi. But before she could decide what to do, they were gone.

Melissa walked into the living room and flopped down on the couch with the remote. She could just veg out to the TV until her parents got home and then go to bed. Mr. and Mrs. Fox always took their time at dinner. It was sure to be dark by the time they got in.

Good plan, Melissa thought, but before she could turn on the television, the front doorbell rang. *Who could that be?* Melissa wondered. If it was Cherie or Gina, she'd just slam the door in their faces. They deserved at least that much. And then she'd figure out how to get back at them in school tomorrow.

But as she approached the door, she felt like kicking herself. Did she honestly think that she was going to swing it open to find one of her friends there? How many times was she going to let herself think they actually cared? It was more likely to be the Publishers Clearing House Prize Patrol with a ten-million-dollar check, or the Avon lady, or a door-to-door salesman demonstrating vacuum cleaners, or—

"*Will?*" Melissa almost choked when she opened the door and saw him standing there, and in the next instant she tried to slam it shut, but Will stuck his foot in the way.

"Ow. Liss—hear me out," he said, talking through the ten inches of space his foot had salvaged.

"We don't have anything to talk about," Melissa snapped. She gave the door a push, but it wouldn't budge.

"Yes, we do," Will protested. "Look—that whole thing with Erika, it was a stupid mistake. From the kiss to the dance . . . all of it."

"What happened? Did she dump you?" Melissa spat.

"No, she didn't *dump* me," Will said, but from his defensive tone, Melissa guessed that she had. Or at the very least, things hadn't turned out the way he wanted them to. Otherwise he'd still be off living his fantasy. That was the way Will was, and Melissa knew it. But whenever things broke down, he always came back to her. The problem was, this time she wasn't sure she wanted him.

"So then, what? She wouldn't make out with you? She wanted to see other people? What?"

"No, it wasn't any of that. She was just . . . boring. She wasn't *you*."

Melissa laughed out loud. "I think that's the lamest line I've ever heard you use," she called through the door.

"It's not a line, Liss—it's true."

Yeah, right, Melissa thought. *If I'm so* not *boring, then why do you keep cheating on me?*

"Come on, Liss. We need each other. You know we do."

Melissa closed her eyes. How many times had she said those very words to him? *Plenty,* she told herself, but that didn't make them true. Still, she stepped back and opened the door, reluctantly meeting Will's gaze. He was standing a step below her, so that for once she didn't have to look up to see him, and somehow his eyes seemed even bluer than normal.

"I don't know, Will," she said, her voice practically a whisper.

"It was a mistake—really, it was, and if I could take it all back, I would."

"But you can't," Melissa breathed.

"No. I can't," Will agreed. "But you could forgive me."

Melissa shook her head. "I'm not sure—"

"I forgave you when you went out with Ken," Will

58

said. "And last night you were with that guy Kurt—"

"*Kel.*"

"Whatever. My point is, I'm willing to give it another shot . . . if you are."

Melissa ran a hand through her long, brown hair and tried to get a grip on all the thoughts running through her head. Sure, she'd gone out with Ken, and Kel too, even if that date hadn't gone anywhere. But both times she and Will had been apart—more or less. He, on the other hand, had cheated on her. Twice now. Was that really something she could get over? Was it something she *should* get over?

"So what do you say?" Will asked. He was practically smiling at her now, like he knew she was going to take him back, and it made Melissa's blood boil. She was just getting ready to tell him to take a flying leap when a car came around the corner—a pale blue Oldsmobile that she knew belonged to Cherie Reese's parents, and Cherie was in the backseat. All at once Melissa made her decision.

"Okay," she said, stepping onto the porch so that he could hug her before Cherie was out of sight. Sure enough, Will wrapped his arms around her, just as she had known he would, and Melissa gave herself over to the hug completely. She rested her head against Will's chest and let his touch comfort her as it had so many times before.

She tried to imagine what Cherie must be thinking right now, after seeing her and Will hugging, and it made her smile. It couldn't have worked out more perfectly. By the time she got to school in the morning, everyone would know that she and Will were back together, and no one would dare to ignore her then—not Cherie, not Gina, not anyone. How could they, when Will's buddies made up the sum total of their dating prospects?

Will rubbed her back with one hand, and Melissa remembered how much she liked it when he held her. True, she wasn't getting back together with him for the best reasons, but it sure beat being alone.

"I'm telling you she's with that . . . *boyfriend* of hers," Mrs. Feldman said, her voice carrying through the open living-room window.

Conner heard the words and froze, his finger two inches from the Feldmans' doorbell. He'd been hoping that maybe Alanna had shown up at her parents' house after all, but obviously she was still missing. And Alanna's parents thought he was to blame.

"Screw this," he mumbled, turning and walking back down the brick steps. Here he'd spent his entire afternoon checking Alanna's favorite hangouts—just to make sure she was okay—and in the meantime her parents were practically accusing him of kidnapping her. Unbelievable.

He swung open the door of his Mustang and slid into the driver's seat, ready to leave the Feldmans to their bickering. But when his hand closed around the key, which was already in the ignition, he paused.

It just didn't make sense. Alanna hadn't been at the Riot or at House of Java. She hadn't been at that secluded part of the beach where she liked to sit on the rocks and watch the ocean. There'd been no sign of her at the movie theater or any of the clubs she went to, and Conner had even checked that freaky fifties diner where they'd had their first date. She didn't seem to be anywhere, and she clearly hadn't come home. So where was she?

Conner leaned his head against the back of his seat and closed his eyes. As much as he hated the idea, he knew he had to talk with Alanna's parents. Maybe there were some relatives nearby that he didn't know about or some old friends he'd never met. Surely her parents would have some idea where she might go. The problem was that as long as they assumed she was with Conner, they weren't going to bother looking any further. Which was why he had to get out of his car and ring that doorbell.

Reluctantly he stumbled back up the walkway and pressed the tiny, white, backlit button. In a matter of seconds Mrs. Feldman flung open the large wooden door and peered out at him through the screen.

"Well, it's about time," she snapped. "Where's my daughter?"

Conner rolled his eyes. "That's why I'm here. I don't know."

Mrs. Feldman folded her arms across her chest and glared at him. "Am I supposed to believe that?"

Conner shook his head. *It's nice to see you too,* he thought.

"Joanna? What is it? Is Alanna back?" Mr. Feldman asked, appearing in the doorway behind her. "Oh. *Conner* . . . hello." The way he said Conner's name, he might as well have been referring to some kind of intestinal flu. Conner nodded in response.

"What's going on here? Where's Alanna?" Mr. Feldman asked in the same accusatory tone his wife had used.

"I don't know," Conner repeated. Maybe one of these times they'd hear him.

Mrs. Feldman clicked her tongue. "Do you honestly expect us to believe that?"

"*Expect?*" Conner said. "No. But if you want to find your daughter, you'd better start believing it."

"I don't think I like your tone, young man," Mr. Feldman said.

"And I don't like your accusations," Conner returned.

They stared at each other for a moment, then the Feldmans exchanged puzzled looks.

"So, then . . . she's really not with you?" Mrs. Feldman said, creasing her brow.

"*No.*"

Mrs. Feldman gasped, and Mr. Feldman put his arm around her. Apparently right up until this moment they'd been expecting her to pop out of Conner's shirt pocket or something.

"Well, then . . . where?" Mrs. Feldman asked. For once her voice was quiet—almost gentle.

"I don't know," Conner said. "I've checked all her usual hangouts. I was hoping you might have some ideas."

"Oh," Mrs. Feldman said. It finally seemed to be hitting her that Alanna was missing. "Well . . ."

"I have one," Mr. Feldman broke in. "I'm calling the police."

"Jake, do you really think—?"

"Joanna, she's gone. You said yourself her duffel bag was missing, and she's not with her boyfriend," he said, waving an arm in Conner's direction.

"Yes, but—"

"No buts. I'm calling." Mr. Feldman turned on his heel and went for the phone. At this point Conner expected Mrs. Feldman to invite him in— at least to the foyer—but instead she just stood

63

there, glancing over her shoulder at her husband.

"Yes, hello. This is Jake Feldman of 1514 Maplewood Drive. I'd like to report my daughter missing." There was a pause, during which Conner figured someone must be transferring Mr. Feldman to another department, and then Mr. Feldman repeated his entire phrase over again. As Conner listened, he couldn't help thinking that Mr. Feldman sounded remarkably calm for someone whose daughter was missing. Then again, as a doctor at a major hospital, he was probably used to keeping his cool in stressful situations.

"Yes," Mr. Feldman went on, "that's right. Seventeen. Yes, this morning. Well, no, but . . . yes . . . yes . . . I see. But isn't there anything—? No. All right . . . yes, thank you. I will."

"Jake? What is it? What are they going to do?" Mrs. Feldman asked.

"Nothing."

Mrs. Feldman drew back. "*Nothing?*"

"They can't," Mr. Feldman said with a shrug. "Apparently she has to be—"

"Missing for twenty-four hours," Conner finished. That knowledge was one of the few things he'd gained from taking off to visit his father in northern California last semester.

"Yes," Mr. Feldman said, nodding at him a bit

suspiciously before turning back to his wife. "So we'll need to call back tomorrow morning."

"If Alanna's not home by then," Mrs. Feldman added.

"Well . . . yes," her husband agreed, though he seemed doubtful Alanna would show up on their doorstep anytime soon.

Twenty-four hours. It seemed like an awfully long time. Alanna could be almost anywhere by then. Still, if they had to wait until morning to report her missing, they might as well make good use of the time.

"Maybe we should—" Conner started.

"*You* should get home," Mrs. Feldman interrupted. "Right now we all need to stay by our phones in case Alanna tries to call." Conner narrowed his eyes. It was a reasonable suggestion, but the way she said it made his temper flare again.

Conner folded his arms across his chest. "Fine," he said with a shrug. Mrs. Feldman's brown eyes softened slightly at his concession. "Good," she said. Conner waited for a moment, glancing first at Mr. Feldman, then at Mrs. Feldman, but it seemed that a "thank you" or "we'll let you know if we hear anything" was too much to expect from Alanna's parents, so he turned to go.

"Just make sure you call us right away if you hear

anything," Mrs. Feldman called after him.

"Anything at all," Mr. Feldman added.

"Uh-huh," Conner said without turning around. *Amazing*, he thought as he swung open the door of his Mustang. He'd come all the way over here to convince them their daughter was missing and that he had nothing to do with it, and they still didn't trust him.

No wonder Alanna had taken off.

Alanna ran her finger along the edge of the silver frame. "I wish you were here," she whispered to Conner's black-and-white image. It was a senior picture she'd managed to wrangle from him, although she hadn't gotten him to sign the back.

She remembered how he'd tossed it to her with a playful smirk. After she'd grabbed it, she had tried to swat him with her hand, but he'd pulled her to him and kissed her instead.

Alanna hugged the picture to her chest. Conner wasn't just her boyfriend—he was her rock. He'd been her only source of stability for the last few months. Alanna sniffed and reached up to wipe away the moisture that was forming in her eyes. As she was bringing down her hand, she caught a flicker of movement across the room and froze. The doorknob was turning.

Alanna's body went rigid. All she could do was stare with horror at the rotating knob. And then, slowly, the door began to open. *Hide,* her brain commanded her, but there was nowhere to go—and there was no time.

This can't be happening, Alanna thought. She'd only been at Lisa's for a few hours now—away from home for less than twenty-four—and already she was about to be caught.

"Hey," Lisa called quietly, sticking her head into the room.

Alanna's heart slid back down to her chest where it belonged, though it was still pounding. "Hey," she breathed.

"What's wrong? Did I scare you?" Lisa asked.

Alanna closed her eyes. *Scare? That's an understatement. More like petrify.*

"Oh my God, I'm so sorry," Lisa said. "I was going to knock, but I thought it might surprise you and make you scream or something."

"That's okay," Alanna said, trying to slow her pulse rate by taking slow, deep breaths. "No big deal." She glanced at the open door nervously. "Where are your parents anyway?"

"They're already asleep," Lisa said, walking in and closing the door behind her. "And their room is downstairs at the other end of the house, so we're pretty safe."

"Oh. Good," Alanna said. She stared down at the

picture of Conner in her lap and traced her finger across his lips.

"Who's that?" Lisa asked, taking a seat next to Alanna on the double bed in Jeff's room.

In spite of everything, Alanna smiled. "Conner," she said, handing the picture to Lisa. "My boyfriend," she added, her entire body warming with the words.

Lisa held up the picture and gazed at it. "*Cute*," she said, glancing at Alanna sideways.

"Mm-hmm. And smart, and funny, and sexy, and sweet—well . . . kind of sweet. In his own way," Alanna said with a slight giggle.

"Wow," Lisa said, raising her eyebrows. "Sounds cool. How long have you been seeing him?"

Alanna shrugged. "A few months, I guess."

"You really like him, huh?" Lisa asked, handing the picture back to Alanna.

"Yeah," Alanna said as she took the photo. She looked it over one more time. Funny. Even though his image was black and white, she could swear Conner's eyes still had a glimmer of green.

"So . . . that's kind of new for you, isn't it?" Lisa asked.

"What?"

"Well, the way I remember it, you were always the heartbreaker—guys fell for you, you dated them for a while, and then you broke up with them."

Alanna squinted. "It wasn't that bad," she said.

"I wasn't saying it was bad," Lisa replied. "Just that you never seemed to be the one who was . . . in love. You know?"

"Yeah." Alanna nodded. She did know. And right up until she'd met Conner, she'd thought that was the way to be. If you weren't in love—or at least not as in love as the other person was with you—you weren't vulnerable, and that was how she'd preferred it. Until Conner.

"So, then . . . don't you want to go back? To where he is, I mean?" Lisa asked, her eyes wide with hope. Alanna's smile faded. Clearly Lisa was still bent on getting her to go home.

"I wish I could," Alanna said. "But there's no way I'm going back to living with my parents." Lisa's eyes dropped, and Alanna sighed. "Look—you don't know how bad things have gotten with my mom and dad. They want to send me off to some kind of prison for girls." Lisa drew back, scrunching up her forehead. "Well, not a prison, exactly," Alanna continued, "but if I hadn't left when I did, they would have had me on a bus to the S. E. Hinton School for Girls or whatever it was called."

"No way," Lisa said. "Your parents wouldn't make you go someplace like that. I mean, I know you haven't always gotten along very well, but what would even make them think of sending you away?"

Alanna blinked and shifted her gaze. Lisa didn't know how serious Alanna's drinking had gotten, and she certainly didn't know about rehab. Mr. and Mrs. Feldman had kept the whole thing so quiet that the only people who did know were a few of Alanna's friends from school, Conner, and anyone he might have told.

"Let's just say it's been a tough year," Alanna said, focusing on the picture of Conner.

"I guess," Lisa said. "I mean, I know your parents have always been kind of strict, but I don't always get along with my parents either. Still, I can't imagine just taking off."

Alanna had to close her eyes to keep herself from rolling them. Lisa's parents probably still held their monthly family meetings just to "check in" with everyone. And they probably still had make-your-own-pizza night every Sunday too. So how could Lisa possibly understand what it was like to live at the Feldmans' house? Her parents probably hadn't ever told her that they'd had it with her or that they wanted to get rid of her by dumping her in some boarding school.

"Lisa," Alanna said, taking a deep breath. "I know I'm putting you in a really hard position, and I'm sorry, but like I said, it's only for a few days. Really. I promise I'll come up with something if you can just buy me a couple of days to think. That's all I need."

Lisa pressed her lips together and scrutinized Alanna's face. "Okay," she said finally. "But then maybe you can talk to my parents about it or something. I know they'd try to help you out—you're practically family."

Alanna put her arm around Lisa's shoulders and gave her a squeeze. "Thanks," she said. "I knew I could count on you." *At least for a few days.* After that, however, Alanna had no idea what she was going to do.

Alanna Feldman

<u>To Do</u>

Find another place to stay. For free. Or at least cheap. I have to make this money last.

Figure out if I'm going to stay in Chicago or move on.

If I'm moving on, I need to figure out where to go.

If I'm going to stay, I have to get a job. Even if I'm really good about spending, this cash won't last forever.

~~Call Conner.~~

~~Write Conner.~~

Think of other friends I could stay with, either in Chicago or somewhere else.

~~Call Conner.~~

Get out of Lisa's house before she breaks down and tells her parents.

Sleep.

Stop thinking about Conner. I'm on my own now, and I've got to take care of myself. He's got his own future to worry about, and I don't want to screw it up for him.

Stop thinking about Conner!!!

Stop crying.

CHAPTER 5

Get Your Priorities Straight

Ken ran the eraser end of his pencil along the bright red locker doors that lined the hallway as he walked toward the guidance office. He'd gotten a note from Mr. Nelson in homeroom excusing him from first period, and now he had a hall pass from Mr. Ford.

But what did Mr. Nelson want with him? He'd finished all his applications long ago, and it was way too early to be hearing from any of the schools now. So, what, then? *Hopefully he doesn't want to put me on another scholarship-judging board,* Ken thought. The Lydia G. Senate experience wasn't one he cared to repeat.

When Ken finally arrived at the guidance office, he didn't even have time to sit down.

"Ken, good. Come right in," Mr. Nelson said, striding through the reception area and into his office.

Shoot, Ken thought. He'd been hoping he'd have to wait awhile—a few minutes at least—so that he could get out of most of history class instead of just the beginning. He followed Mr. Nelson and took a

75

seat in one of the black leather chairs facing his desk.

"So . . . what's up?" Ken asked when Mr. Nelson was seated.

Mr. Nelson gazed at him with somber eyes. "I'm afraid I have some bad news," he said.

Ken cringed. *Great. He has heard from the schools I applied to, and I didn't get into any of them.*

"It's not insurmountable," Mr. Nelson continued, "but you're still not going to like it."

"What is it?" Ken asked.

"Well, it seems that when you were a sophomore, you were failing math—a combined geometry/algebra II with Ms. Knight?"

"*Yeah,*" Ken said, leaning forward.

"And it seems that your guidance counselor at the time—Mr. Tingley, was it?"

"Mm-hmm." Ken nodded, remembering what a space case Mr. Tingley was. He hadn't seemed qualified to offer *anyone* guidance. It was no wonder that year had been his first and last at Sweet Valley.

"Yes, well, it seems Mr. Tingley arranged for you to switch into an accounting class—which you aced. A ninety-eight average for the year. That's pretty good." He paused to smile at Ken, which only served to make Ken uncomfortable.

"Thanks," he said, shifting in his seat and focusing

76

on the various diplomas and certificates hanging on Mr. Nelson's wall.

"But there is a problem," Mr. Nelson said. "One that I'm afraid Mr. Tingley overlooked and no one else thought of at the time." Ken's palms were beginning to feel clammy. Could he just get to the point already?

Mr. Nelson cleared his throat. "You see, while the accounting class satisfied your math requirements here at Sweet Valley High, it turns out that it doesn't satisfy the entrance requirements of most universities. In fact, it doesn't satisfy the requirements for any of the schools to which you applied."

Ken shook his head. "You mean . . . wait. What are you saying?"

Mr. Nelson breathed deeply. "What I'm saying is that all of the schools you applied to require high-school geometry or some basic equivalent, just as they require at least two years of a foreign language and four years of English."

"But . . . so, then . . . where does that leave me?" Ken asked. "Can I drop, I don't know, history and take geometry now or what?"

"Unfortunately, it's too late in the year to get into a geometry class, but—"

"You're kidding me," Ken said. This couldn't be happening. He'd spent most of last night trying to convince himself that his father was wrong. That he could go to a good school and get by. More than get by—actually do well. But now it turned out he wasn't even qualified to apply at most colleges, let alone be considered for acceptance.

"I wish I was," Mr. Nelson said. "But unfortunately Mr. Tingley made a bad choice for you, and no one caught it until now. I'm sorry, Ken. I wish I'd seen it before. I was alerted by the schools' administrators after they received your complete transcripts. Still, you do have options."

"Yeah, right," Ken said. "Like what?" He could just imagine. Taking a semester off or more likely a whole year to finish his math requirement and then applying all over again? And just what would he do for a year? Live at home with his dad and work at the grocery store or something? Oh, yeah, his dad would just love that. It would definitely prove him right— that Ken wasn't capable of doing anything without some kind of special help. Like a bribe to a football scout. Or some kind of sports scholarship.

"Actually, I'm afraid I don't have the answers now. I just wanted to make you aware of the situation and let you know that I'm looking into it. I'm sure, given a few days to check around, that I can come up with a solution that will still allow you to—"

"Forget it," Ken muttered, standing.

"Now, Ken. I'm sure we can find—"

"No, really," Ken said, turning away. "Don't waste your time. I'll just do the rolling application at the community college. It's where I belong anyway."

"Don't be ridiculous, Ken. Community college is a fine option, but I'm sure we can provide you with some other choices as well."

"Oh, yeah," Ken said, without stopping. "I forgot about correspondence courses."

"Ken—"

"No," Ken said, turning to face Mr. Nelson. "Forget it. Really. I don't even want to talk about it. I know where I belong, and it's definitely not at UCLA or any of those other stupid schools you had me apply to. So just leave me alone. I'll figure something out."

He stalked out of the guidance office. If Mr. Nelson thought he could help by filling Ken's head full of more impossible ideas about what he was capable of, he had another think coming. Because now Ken knew exactly what he was capable of. Nothing. And he didn't need any more illusions about how bright his future was.

His father was right. He'd been right all along. Without a free ride on a football team, college was out of Ken's reach. And the sooner he faced up to that, the better.

"Walk me to gym after?" Melissa asked, tilting her head and gazing up at Will.

"Sure. I'll meet you by the door," Will answered, leaning down to give her a brief kiss. Melissa smiled at him as adoringly as she possibly could—everyone was watching, after all—then grabbed her tray from the lunch counter and proceeded to the table where all of her friends were already waiting.

That went as well as it could, she thought, forcing herself to maintain a steady gait and trying to appear nonchalant. Now, if she could just get through twenty minutes of lunchtime gossip, she'd be all set.

"Hi," she said, setting down her tray and taking the free seat next to Gina. A silence fell over the table, but Melissa pretended not to notice. "Great dance Friday night, huh?" she asked with a giggle. There was no sense trying to avoid the topic. Besides, it was best to tackle these things head-on—that was the only way to gain an advantage.

Cherie's eyes were wide. She was staring at Melissa, speechless, and she wasn't the only one. Gina was staring too. And while neither Lila nor Amy would meet Melissa's eyes, it was clear how uncomfortable they were by the way they were both poking at their food and moving the vegetables around on their plates. But that was all right. Melissa knew exactly what to say.

"Okay. So I was a little out of control. But Kel didn't seem to mind," she said with a smirk. "Of

80

course, he did insist on grabbing some coffee before we headed back to his fraternity house," she added casually. "I guess he wanted to make sure I knew what I was doing."

Amy dropped her fork. "You went back to his frat house?"

"*Fraternity,*" Melissa corrected her. "They're really sensitive about that."

"Okay, *fraternity* house," Amy said. "But still— did you seriously go there with him? Alone?"

Melissa forced herself to laugh even though she knew this was the risky part. If Jessica had spilled anything about what really happened, Melissa was going to have some serious trouble digging herself out of this one.

"*Yes,* I really went with him. What's the big deal?"

"Nothing. I mean, it's just that . . ." Amy held Melissa's gaze for a moment, then faltered. She picked up her fork and started rearranging her carrots again.

"It's just that you were pretty out of it," Gina finished for her. *Oh, so you did notice,* Melissa thought, glancing around the table. Yet not one of them had even tried to stop her.

Melissa shrugged. "Maybe a little. But like I said, Kel made sure I had time to sober up before he asked me back to the house. And when I said yes, I knew exactly what I was doing."

"And just what *did* you do?" Cherie asked, her eyebrows shooting upward.

Again Melissa laughed, but this time it was genuine. Obviously none of her friends knew the truth about what had happened Friday night, which was a huge relief. Not to mention that it was kind of fun to watch their reactions to her lies about Kel. "Not much, really," she said. "We just went up to his room and fooled around for a while, and then he drove me home."

"Wow," Amy said, finally managing to meet Melissa's eyes again. "He was *so* hot. I bet he was a good kisser."

Melissa smirked, but she didn't comment. She didn't need to. At this point it was better to let them fill in the details on their own. Instead she shoved a spoonful of yogurt into her mouth and waited. But she didn't have to wait long.

"What about Will?" Lila asked, her eyes darting toward Cherie. *Good,* Melissa thought. *Cherie did get the rumor started.* Not that she'd expected Cherie to let an opportunity for good gossip slip by. "Are you guys back together or what?" Lila continued.

Melissa paused before answering. It was the question she had been waiting for. She glanced over at Will's table, where he and his friends were talking animatedly about something—probably football or basketball—and smiled. "Yeah, I guess we are," she said.

"And what does he think about you messing around with Kel?" Cherie asked.

Melissa shrugged. "He was a little jealous, but I think he's okay with it now."

"So you told him everything?" Gina asked.

"Pretty much," Melissa said. "He came over yesterday to let me know he'd cut Erika loose and ask me what was up with Kel. So I told him."

"What did he say?" Amy asked.

"He was kind of upset at first," Melissa said. "But then he said he didn't care what had happened. He just wanted to get back together. So we talked about it, and I finally decided that even though it was fun to play around with someone else for a while, in the end Will's the one who's always there for me. And there's something kind of nice about that. So I said yes, and now we're together again."

"Wow," Amy said. She took a bite of her chicken sandwich and swallowed quickly. "Your weekend sure beat mine."

"Mine too," Gina agreed. "I went straight home after the dance and spent Sunday doing homework."

"Me too," Lila said.

"So," Amy started, glancing around the table, then focusing on Melissa. "Is Kel seeing anyone else right now?" she asked with a grin, and everyone laughed.

*   *   *

Conner walked across the parking lot, squinting against the bright sun. The next thing to do was to check with Alanna's friends. The problem was, he barely knew them.

What was that girl's name anyway? Conner asked himself. The one Alanna had introduced him to just a couple of weeks ago. Maria? No, Marissa—that was it. Marissa . . . *Polland.* And Alanna had said she lived somewhere near Ocean Park, but Conner had no idea where. He'd just have to call her. He'd looked her up in the phone book once and knew her number was listed. With that plan in mind, he headed for his car. And he was so busy congratulating himself for remembering all of that information that he didn't hear Tia and Andy until they were practically on top of him.

"Conner!" Tia yelled. "What's wrong with you anyway? We've been yelling your name all the way across the parking lot. Didn't you hear us?"

Conner's muscles tensed.

"Seriously," Andy chimed in. "You must be focused, McD. What's up? And where have you been all day? I've barely seen you—except in Quigley's class. That essay test was brutal. How'd you do?"

"Okay," Conner said, though he really didn't remember much of what he'd written. His mind hadn't exactly been on writing.

Damn, he thought. If he'd been just ten seconds faster getting out of school, he could have been in his car and pulling away before they'd caught up to him. But now he was stuck—and after having avoided the two of them all day too. That's what he got for letting his guard down too soon.

"Hey—we're going for coffee. Want to come?" Tia asked.

"Nah. I've got other stuff to do," Conner said, and with anyone else, that would have been enough of an explanation. But not with Tia.

"Like what?" she asked.

"Just . . . stuff," Conner said, staring off into the distance. He really didn't want to get into the whole Alanna situation right now. He didn't have time. "I'll see you later," he said, heading for his car, but Tia wouldn't let up.

"What's going on?" she asked, following him. "Is something wrong?"

"No," Conner said just as he reached his car. He grabbed the door handle and swung his bag into the backseat, then got ready to slide behind the wheel.

"So then why won't you even look at me?" Tia demanded. Conner stopped and turned his head toward her, glaring. "Cute." Tia cocked her head. "But I'm not letting you go until you tell me what's up." Conner sighed and shrugged.

"She really won't, you know," Andy said. "And I've seen her hold back cars before. It's not pretty."

Conner closed the door to his car and leaned up against it. "Okay. Look. I didn't want to get into this, but . . . Alanna's missing."

"Missing?" Tia said, scrunching her eyebrows together. "Like, gone?"

"Yeah," Conner said.

"You mean, she ran away?" Andy asked, his eyes widening. Conner nodded. "When?"

"Saturday, I guess. Her parents didn't notice until Sunday morning, so she probably left while they were asleep."

"And they don't know where she is?" Tia asked.

"Nope," Conner said, turning to open his car door once again.

"Wow," Tia said. For once she seemed to be at a loss for words, which made it a perfect time to take off. Conner slid in behind the steering wheel and turned his key in the ignition, then rolled down his window to say good-bye.

"I'll see you guys later," he said, getting ready to back up. But before he could, Tia was at his side again.

"Wait a second," she said, poking her head through the window. "This is Monday."

"*Yeah*," Conner said.

"So . . . don't you have a lesson with Gavin?"

Conner rolled his eyes. Sometimes Tia was worse than his mother. Or even his sister. "Yeah. So?"

"So are you going?" she asked, piercing him with her brown eyes.

"No," Conner said, and he threw his arm over the backseat and turned his head to look out the back window.

"Conner!" Tia said. "You can't skip your guitar lesson. You've got that audition on Wednesday. You need to practice."

Conner turned back to Tia and narrowed his eyes. Was she serious? How was he supposed to even think about anything else when Alanna was missing? She could be anywhere. She could be in serious trouble, and he was supposed to go play scales and practice riffs? He glanced over Tia's shoulder at Andy, who just shrugged helplessly. He obviously wasn't going to interfere, but he wasn't going to drag Tia off Conner's car either.

"I don't need to practice," he said evenly. "I need to find Alanna."

"Oh, come on, Conner," Tia said. "Don't be so dramatic. I'm sure she's fine. She's probably already home. But even if she isn't, you have to focus on your audition. You can't go running all over town looking for her. This audition could be a major part of your future."

Conner shook his head and scowled at her. Tia might mean well, but as far as he was concerned, her priorities were all screwed up.

"Yeah, whatever," he said, shifting into reverse and backing up. He went slowly at first, so that Tia would back away, and then increased his speed. Once he was sure he was clear of her, he swung the car around hard and peeled out, leaving Tia, Andy, and a thick layer of rubber behind.

My future, huh? he thought as he pulled out of the SVH parking lot. What about Alanna's? Or didn't she deserve one?

TIA RAMIREZ

WHAT'S THAT EXPRESSION? "LOVE IS BLIND"? WELL, IT'S DEAF AND DUMB TOO. CONNER DIDN'T HEAR A WORD I SAID, AND GETTING HIM TO TALK ABOUT ALANNA—OR ANY OF HIS RELATIONSHIPS, FOR THAT MATTER—IS VIRTUALLY IMPOSSIBLE.

I CAN'T BELIEVE HE'S THROWING AWAY HIS SHOT AT GETTING INTO SUCH A COOL COLLEGE JUST TO GO LOOK FOR ALANNA. WHAT IS HE THINKING? AND WHAT WAS <u>SHE</u> THINKING TAKING OFF LIKE THAT ANYWAY? OBVIOUSLY NOT OF CONNER, OR SHE WOULDN'T HAVE DONE IT. AT LEAST NOT WHEN HE'S GOT SUCH AN AMAZING OPPORTUNITY IN FRONT OF HIM.

THEN AGAIN, THE AUDITION ISN'T UNTIL WEDNESDAY, SO HE HASN'T BLOWN IT YET. AND HE

WON'T, IF I HAVE ANYTHING TO SAY ABOUT IT. OF COURSE, GETTING THROUGH TO SOMEONE WHO'S DEAF, DUMB, AND BLIND ISN'T GOING TO BE EASY.

MAYBE I'D BETTER GO REREAD <u>THE MIRACLE WORKER.</u>

One More Letdown

6

"Hi . . . Marissa?" Conner said.

"*Yeah*—who's this?"

"Conner. Conner McDermott. We talked once, when I was worried about Alanna."

"Oh—*Conner*," Marissa said. "How are you?"

"Uh, fine. Actually, I was calling to see if you'd heard from Alanna."

"*Heard* from her? What do you mean? I saw her in school on Friday," she offered. It was obvious she didn't have a clue that Alanna was missing. Stupid Feldmans. What had they been doing all day? Hadn't they contacted anyone?

"I mean since then," Conner explained. "Like, did you talk to her on the phone over the weekend or anything? Or has she e-mailed you since Saturday?"

There was a silence while Marissa thought his question over. "No, I guess not. And she wasn't in school today either. Why? What's going on?"

Conner pressed his eyes shut. If the Feldmans

weren't so concerned about their standing at the country club, Marissa would know by now. Everyone would, and they could all be looking for Alanna. If something happened to her because of their hesitation, he was never going to let them hear the end of it.

"She's missing," Conner said.

"What do you mean, 'missing'?"

"Nobody's seen her since Saturday night—not her parents, not anyone at any of the clubs where she hangs out. No one. I was hoping maybe you'd have some idea where she might be."

"Oh, wow," Marissa said. "Well . . . did you check that little café-bookstore in town? I know she couldn't stay there overnight or anything, but I've seen her spend hours there before when she needed to get away from the house for a while."

"Yeah, I checked it out. She wasn't there, and the guy at the counter worked all weekend and he was pretty sure she hadn't been in."

"Oh, man. I don't know, then. I mean, Jill and Dan and I are really the only people she hangs out with, and even though we all know her parents suck, I don't see how she could stay at any of our houses without our parents calling the Feldmans."

"Yeah," Conner agreed. "What about someone out of town, though? Hey—" he said, suddenly remembering something Alanna had mentioned once

92

about her best friend from grade school. "Doesn't she have a friend in Chicago? Someone who moved away her freshman or sophomore year?"

"Oh, yeah—Lisa," Marissa said. "Lisa Bresinsky. They were best friends."

"Do you know how I can get in touch with her?"

"Yeah, hold on a second. I think I have her number somewhere," Marissa said. Conner heard the receiver clunk on the floor and listened as Marissa's footsteps padded away. In a minute he heard her come back.

"Okay—here it is," she said.

Conner listened carefully and wrote down the number, repeating it back to Marissa before hanging up. Then, without wasting a minute, he punched in the numbers and waited. After just two rings there was an answer.

"Hello?"

"Hi. Lisa?"

"*Yes* . . . ," the girl answered, and to Conner, she already sounded wary. Like someone who was hiding something.

His heart sped up. If he was right, and Alanna had gone to Lisa for help, he needed to make sure he played it cool. He didn't want Lisa hanging up before he could figure out whether or not she knew anything.

"This is Conner, Conner McDermott. I'm a friend of Alanna's. Her boyfriend, actually," he added at the last minute, sensing it might help.

"Oh, hi," Lisa said.

"I know this might sound weird," he started, "but I was wondering if you'd heard from Alanna recently."

"Recently?" Lisa repeated. "Well . . . no. Not really. I mean, we write back and forth and she calls every once in a while, but recently? I guess not. Why?"

Liar, Conner thought. Her shaky voice and the length of her answer practically confirmed she knew something.

"Huh. So she hasn't been in touch with you?" Conner persisted. "Not at all?"

"Well, not recently," Lisa repeated. "Why?"

"Because she's missing," Conner said. "And nobody seems to know where she is."

"Oh. Wow. That's terrible," Lisa said. She spoke in the slow staccato of an unrehearsed—and very bad—actor.

"Yeah, it is," Conner agreed. "I'm really worried about her, and—now that you know—I'm sure you are too."

"Of course I am," Lisa replied. "But like I said, I haven't seen her."

"That's too bad," Conner said, "because I was really thinking that Chicago was where I would find her. But if you think that's a dead end . . . ," he said, letting his voice trail off.

"Well, I wouldn't rule it out," she said finally. "I mean, just because *I* haven't seen her, that doesn't mean—well, you know. Chicago's a big city."

"Yeah, it is," Conner agreed. "So you think maybe she could be there somewhere?" Lisa didn't respond right away, and for a moment Conner thought she had hung up. "Lisa? Are you still there?"

"Yeah. I'm here," she said quietly.

"Look, I'm really concerned about Alanna," Conner said. "I just want to make sure she's all right and help her out if she needs it. I don't know if she's ever mentioned me or not, but . . . I'd really like to find her. But if you can tell me Chicago's a dead end, I'll forget about it and start looking somewhere else."

Again there was silence. But just as Conner was about to prompt her, Lisa spoke.

"I can't tell you that," she said. And then she hung up.

When Ken walked into the kitchen and saw his father sitting at the table, reading the paper, his spirits deflated. *Not tonight,* he thought.

The only time Mr. Matthews ever sat at the kitchen table in the evening to read the paper was when he was waiting to have one of his talks with

Ken, and tonight Ken definitely wasn't in the mood. Especially since it would probably be about college.

After what Mr. Nelson had said that morning, college wasn't in Ken's future. At least not the kind of college experience that either Ken or his dad had in mind. Of course, Ken had no intention of letting his father in on that bit of news anytime soon. He had to figure out what he was going to do first and where else he might be able to live if he did go the community-college route.

"Ken, have a seat," Mr. Matthews said, folding his paper. Ken wondered why his father even bothered with the whole newspaper charade. They both knew he'd already read it at breakfast, not to mention the fact that he *worked* at the *Trib*. And just how many times did he need to go over the news in one day, anyway?

"Actually, Dad, I've got a lot of homework tonight, so I think I'll just head upstairs and get started," Ken said, breezing through the kitchen. He was halfway to the stairs when he heard his father's voice.

"I had an interesting talk with Mr. Nelson today," Mr. Matthews said from the kitchen, stopping Ken. "He called me at work." Ken closed his eyes and let his head drop to his chest. Just when he'd thought things couldn't get any worse.

Slowly he turned and walked back to the kitchen. "So

you know," he said without meeting his father's eyes.

"About your math requirement? Yes," Mr. Matthews said. "But what I don't understand is why you stormed out of Mr. Nelson's office. He was very concerned about you. He said you didn't even let him finish explaining everything."

"What else was there to explain?" Ken asked, folding his arms across his chest. "I don't have enough math to get into college, and it's too late to take the class. I'm screwed. Did he think I didn't understand that?"

"Ken, this attitude will get you nowhere, so I suggest you drop it right now," Mr. Matthews said, rising from his chair. He walked to the sink and filled a glass with water, then turned and leaned against the counter, facing his son.

Ken clenched his teeth. He didn't want to look his father in the eye, but he couldn't help himself—it was like trying to avoid staring at the scene of an accident. And sure enough, when he let his gaze meet his father's, Ken saw exactly what he had expected to see. Disappointment. His dad's blue eyes appeared flat gray, and they seemed to droop right into his sagging cheeks. It was the face of an old man who'd been let down so much that he'd come to expect it, as though each new disappointment was just another one to add to the pile.

"So? What do you plan to do about this?" Mr. Matthews asked.

"*Do?*" Ken echoed. "What *can* I do? I'm just going to enroll at the community college in town and go from there."

"Be serious," Mr. Matthews commanded him.

"I am," Ken insisted.

His father shook his head. "You can't go to community college—it's beneath you."

"Beneath me? It's the only thing I'm qualified for."

"That's not true. You were offered a perfectly good scholarship to the University of Michigan, so you can certainly do better than community college."

"You *bought* me that one, Dad," Ken snapped. "It hardly counts."

"Of course it counts—it was a good opportunity, and I'm sure you can find others if you just look around. And talk to Mr. Nelson, for goodness' sake. He can tell you what you need to do to—"

"To what?" Ken asked. "To keep from embarrassing you?"

Mr. Matthews drew back. "That's certainly not what I was going to say."

"Yeah, but it's what you were thinking. Admit it. The only reason you don't want me to go to community college is because it would be embarrassing for *you*. You can't stand the idea of having to tell people that your loser son is taking classes in town instead of playing football for Notre Dame, can you?"

"Ken, don't be ridiculous. You can't—"

"I'm not being ridiculous. I'm serious."

"So you're not even planning to talk things over with Mr. Nelson?"

"Why should I? I've got it all figured out," Ken said.

Mr. Matthews shook his head. "Well, at least it's reassuring to see that you're handling this in your typical manner. Then again, once a quitter, always a quitter."

Suddenly anger flared in Ken's chest, and he felt his face redden. "You think I'm a quitter? Fine. I'm not going to college at all. How's that for quitting?" He glared at his father just long enough to see his jaw muscles tense, then he turned and stalked out of the room.

Who needed college anyway? Certainly not him. He probably never would have gotten a degree anyway. After all, he couldn't even get through high-school geometry.

"You're kidding," Lisa's voice boomed from somewhere down the hall. "Are you seriously going to change the sheets on Jeff's bed right now?"

Right now? Alanna thought, jumping out of the desk chair she'd been lounging in. *Oh, no.* She heard Mrs. Bresinsky's muffled voice and then Lisa talking way too loud again.

"But he's not coming home for another couple of weeks." Again Mrs. Bresinsky's voice could be heard—still muffled, but definitely getting closer.

I've got to get out of here, Alanna thought, glancing around the room nervously. Then she saw the door to the back stairs—the ones that led down to the garage. It was the only way. Quickly she darted over to the bed and grabbed her duffel bag, then ran—on her toes—to the door. She pulled it open as quietly as possible and crept through, pulling it closed at precisely the same moment that she heard the other door open.

"You're so neurotic about housework," Lisa said.

"Lisa—what's wrong with you? When did you become so concerned about my sheet-changing habits? And why are you talking like that?"

"Like what?" Lisa said, still a few notches above normal speaking volume.

There was a pause, and Alanna heard feet coming closer to the door. She sucked in her breath, certain that she was about to be discovered, but then the footsteps stopped. "Never mind," Mrs. Bresinsky said, and Alanna heard the sound of blankets being stripped from the bed. Obviously Lisa's mother was busy changing the sheets, which meant the feet that had stopped at the other side of the door were Lisa's.

Good idea, Alanna thought, realizing that her

friend had placed herself between Mrs. Bresinsky and the door. But just when Alanna was beginning to relax a bit, she was jarred by another sound—the automatic-garage-door opener. Mr. Bresinsky was pulling in, and his timing couldn't have been any worse.

Alanna had come down to the fourth step, but now she stole back up to the top. As gently as possible, she pressed her back against the door, taking great care not to jar it. In that position she should be completely out of Mr. Bresinsky's view. Unless, of course, he came around to the passenger side of the car for some reason. But why would he do that? *He wouldn't*, Alanna told herself, willing it not to happen.

"Hmmm," she heard Mrs. Bresinsky say. "I wonder who this is. I don't remember seeing this picture before." Alanna's eyes nearly popped out of her head when she realized what Lisa's mother was talking about. Her picture of Conner—she'd left it on Jeff's desk.

"Oh, that's, uh, Conner," Lisa said, affecting an almost casual tone. "He's new in Jeff's dorm this semester. Jeff just brought it home during winter break."

Not bad, Alanna thought. *Except why would a guy his brother just met be giving him a framed picture?*

"Why would a boy Jeff just met give him a framed picture?" Mrs. Bresinsky asked. Alanna heard her set the frame back down on Jeff's desk and get back to the business of making the bed.

"I don't know," Lisa said. "Maybe he has a crush on Jeff."

Mrs. Bresinsky laughed and Alanna breathed half a sigh of relief. She was waiting on the other half until she heard Mr. Bresinsky go inside. She could hear his footsteps on the concrete floor, and thankfully they seemed headed away from her. In another minute she heard him open the door to the kitchen, and then she heard it shut, but she still didn't dare to let her breath out. Not until Mrs. Bresinsky was gone too.

"Here, let me get this side," she heard Lisa offer.

It was silent for a moment except for the sound of rustling blankets and sheets, then finally Alanna heard Mrs. Bresinsky say, "There. Done for now."

Alanna heard Mrs. Bresinsky gathering up all the old sheets and heading for the hall, but Lisa seemed to be standing next to the door again. At least she hoped it was Lisa at the door and not the other way around.

"Well, come on," Mrs. Bresinsky said. "You know you can't stay in Jeff's room when he's not here. We have to respect his privacy."

"Oh. Yeah. Sorry," Lisa said. "I was just thinking about something that happened in school today."

"Anything you want to talk about?" Alanna heard Mrs. Bresinsky ask as Lisa's footsteps grew softer and softer. She could hear them talking in the hall even after the door to Jeff's room was shut, but their voices were muffled. And distant, thank God.

Carefully Alanna turned the doorknob and let herself back into Jeff's room, walking straight to her picture of Conner and hugging it close. "You almost got me into trouble that time," she whispered quietly. "That's a first." Usually Conner was the one coming to her rescue. Lisa had covered for her this time. But what if she hadn't?

She knew Lisa had been reluctant to lie to her parents from the beginning, and if she'd been half as shaken up by what just happened as Alanna had, she wasn't going to be doing it much longer. Which meant that after only twenty-four hours with Lisa, it was already time for Alanna to move on again. There was just one problem. *Where?*

Ken Matthews

Benjamin Franklin, Thomas Edison, and Mark Twain never even went to high school. And then there are a ton of famous people—like Jim Carrey, Quentin Tarantino, Joe DiMaggio, Casey Stengel, Tom Cruise—who never finished high school. That's <u>high school</u>. Forget about college. They never even bothered.

So it seems like if you're destined for greatness, you're going to get there whether you have a high-school diploma and a college degree or not. Which makes me think that it must work the same in the other direction too. Like, if you're destined to be a loser, nothing you do is going to change that. Not high school, not college, not a football scholarship, nothing.

So the way I see it, the best thing for me to do is just accept my destiny now. And if that's the same as just giving up, then I guess my father's right. I _am_ a quitter. But what's the point in trying when you already know you're going to fail? That just seems stupid.

CHAPTER
The Perfect Plan
7

"Hey! Marsden," Conner called, catching up with Andy just outside his homeroom.

Andy turned, his eyebrows raised. "Conner. What's up? Did you find Alanna?"

"No," Conner said, glancing over Andy's shoulder just in time to see Tia headed their way. "Come here," he muttered to Andy, nodding toward the end of the hall. Andy shot a quick look at Tia, hesitated, then turned and followed Conner. And, as Conner had hoped she would, Tia got the hint and headed for her locker instead of joining them.

"So what's going on?" Andy asked. "You seem pretty tense. I mean, more so than usual," he added with a half grin.

"I need to borrow some money," Conner told him. "Enough for a plane ticket to Chicago."

Andy screwed up his face. "Chicago?" he blurted out. "What do you need in Chicago?"

"That's where Alanna is. At least, I'm pretty sure she is."

"That's great—you found her," Andy exclaimed, clapping Conner on the shoulder. But then his scowl returned. "But why do you need to go out there? I mean, shouldn't her parents be doing that?"

Conner shrugged.

"Oh, no," Andy said, taking a step back. "You haven't told them, have you? You haven't told anyone. The Feldmans, your mom." Conner stared at the ceiling and waited for Andy to finish putting it all together. "And now what? You're going to go to Chicago and bring her back yourself?"

And there it is, Conner thought, feeling like he should be offering Andy some kind of cheesy game-show prize.

"What are you—crazy?" Andy went on. "You can't just take off to Chicago. For one thing, you at least need to tell Alanna's parents where she is. And for another, you've got that audition tomorrow. What are you going to do—skip it?"

"You're just as bad as Tia," Conner told him. "Don't you get that Alanna could be in trouble?"

"Of course we do. But Conner—come on, man. You can't just skip out on your audition. You may not get another chance."

"Yeah, well, I happen to think Alanna's life is a little

more important than playing a few songs for a stuck-up music professor."

Andy held up his palms like little stop signs. "Hey—I'm not saying it isn't. I'm just saying, maybe you should let her parents handle this."

"Oh, right. Mr. and Mrs. Hospitality," Conner scoffed. "If Alanna saw them coming, she'd be on the first plane to Czechoslovakia."

Andy sighed. "Look, man, I wish I could help you out," he said. "But even if I thought going to Chicago was the right thing to do, I just don't have that kind of money."

Conner shot him a stony glare. "Yeah. Okay."

"Really. I don't," Andy insisted, but Conner just turned and walked away.

"Whatever," he said, raising one hand toward Andy without looking back. He knew Andy must have a savings account, or a college fund, or something his parents had probably started for him years ago. And if he really wanted to, he could get the money. Conner was sure of it.

Andy just didn't understand the kind of trouble Alanna could be in right now. No one did. Except for Conner. And that was because he'd been there himself.

"Where's Will?" Cherie asked when Melissa fell into line behind her in the cafeteria.

Melissa smirked. It was amazing how quickly things could shift in high school. Just a few days ago Cherie wouldn't have dreamed of asking Melissa about Will, and now here she was, acting like he and Melissa had never split at all.

"Computer lab," Melissa answered, taking a tray from the buffet cart. "He had to finish writing something up for physics."

"Bummer," Cherie said.

Melissa shrugged. It was no great loss to her, although she certainly would have enjoyed the chance to cozy up to him in front of her friends again—just in case they missed anything yesterday at lunch. Or after school. Or this morning in homeroom. "He probably would have sat with his friends anyway," she said.

"Yeah," Cherie said wistfully, and Melissa noticed she was gazing toward the table where Will's friends were already seated. And if Melissa was right, she was staring at one person in particular.

"How are things going with Aaron?" Melissa asked, sliding her tray across the metal buffet table and snagging a salad bowl.

Cherie blew a puff of air toward her forehead, making her auburn bangs flutter. "I wish I knew," she said.

"What do you mean?" Melissa asked. "You went to the dance with him, didn't you?"

"Yeah, but . . ." Cherie shook her head. "I don't know.

We were with a whole group of people, you know?"

Yes, I remember, Melissa thought. *The group I wasn't invited to join.* But even as she thought it, she willed herself to nod understandingly and keep the bitterness out of her voice. "Uh-huh," she said, encouraging Cherie to continue.

"So it was like all eight of us were out together, not like Aaron and I were on a date or anything. I mean, I had a good time, and I think he did too, but I'm just not sure if he'd want to go out again or not. I mean, with just me—you know?"

"Yeah, that's the thing about group dates," Melissa said. "It's hard to figure out where you stand." She lifted a bunch of lettuce into her bowl, then plunked in a few tomatoes and cucumbers.

"Exactly," Cherie said. "I just wish there was some way I could find out whether or not he likes me."

Melissa topped off her salad with some shredded carrots as her mind worked double time. Obviously Cherie had it pretty bad for Aaron. So if she could find some way to sabotage their relationship, keep it from ever happening, that would be payback enough for Cherie. But only if Cherie knew Melissa was behind it—otherwise it would just seem like bad luck. And it still left the problem of Will. If only there was some way she could get back at both of them at once.

"I hate dating," Cherie moaned from the other side

111

of the salad cart. "You're so lucky you have a boyfriend."

Yeah, right, Melissa thought, *and he's such a prize.* Then it hit her. *Will. Of course.* It was so obvious, she wondered why she hadn't seen it before.

"You know," she said, glancing over at Cherie, "maybe there is a way you can figure out what's going on with Aaron." She picked up her tray and moved it to the next section.

"Really? How?" Cherie asked, trailing behind with her empty lunch tray at her side.

"Aren't you getting anything to eat?" Melissa asked.

"I'm not really hungry," Cherie said with a shrug, and Melissa smirked again. *It must be love,* she mused. "I'll just snag a yogurt or something," Cherie added. "But what do you mean, 'maybe there is a way'? Do you have an idea?"

Cherie's eyes were so wide with hope, it was pathetic. Didn't she have a clue how vulnerable she was? *Obviously not,* Melissa told herself, *or she'd at least try to show a little restraint.* She was almost making things too easy.

"Well, nothing brilliant," Melissa said, "but maybe I could get Will to talk him—you know, discreetly. Just to find out if he's interested."

"That would be perfect," Cherie said. "As long as you think Will can do it without making it sound like I asked him to."

112

"I'm sure he can. He's pretty good at that stuff. And besides, you won't be asking him to do it. I will. So you're in the clear."

Cherie's mouth curved into a wide grin, and she looked so grateful that for a moment Melissa thought she was going to hug her. "Thanks, Melissa," she said, grabbing an apple from the fruit cart. "You're such a good friend. I'm so glad things worked out between you and Will."

Melissa nodded and smiled. *Mm-hmm. Of course you are,* she thought. But she was pretty sure Cherie would be feeling differently in the not too distant future.

After all, considering how she felt about Aaron, she was probably going to be pretty devastated to see him hooking up with one of her friends. And if that friend just happened to be Melissa, well, then Will would get a little of his own back too, wouldn't he?

"How about, *'Donde están mis pantalones?'*" Andy said.

Tia pressed her lips together. "Okay. For one thing, that's Spanish," she said.

"I know." Andy smiled proudly. "Evan taught it to me."

"*Bueno,*" Tia said. "But this is *French* class."

"Mademoiselle Ramirez? Monsieur Marsden? *Est-ce*

qu'il y a un problème?" Ms. Dalton asked, looking up from her desk.

"*Non,* Madame Dalton," Tia answered, glaring at Andy. "So are you ready to be serious now?" she asked him, keeping her voice down.

"Yeah, I guess—oh! That reminds me," Andy started. "I've been meaning to tell you what Conner asked me this morning."

"Oh, yeah," Tia said, remembering the glare Conner had shot her after homeroom. "He's pretty upset with me, huh?"

"Probably, but that's not what he wanted to talk to me about," Andy said.

"What, then?" Tia asked.

"He wanted to know if I could lend him money to get a plane ticket to Chicago."

"*What?*" Tia practically yelled, attracting Ms. Dalton's attention again. "I mean, '*pourquoi?*' That's what we should have Philippe say right here," she added, tapping the paper and mouthing "sorry" to Ms. Dalton.

"Why does he need a plane ticket to Chicago?" Tia whispered. "Oh, wait—don't tell me. That's where Alanna is." Andy nodded. "What is he thinking?" Tia asked.

"I don't know," Andy said, "but I told him I didn't have that kind of money to lend."

"Well, that's good, at least. Hopefully he hasn't found someone else to give it to him."

114

"I doubt it," Andy said. "But it wouldn't surprise me if he was trying to figure out how long it would take him to drive there."

Tia shook her head. "We've got to do something," she said, "or he's going to screw up his life trying to get her home."

"Yeah, but what? He's not exactly keen on taking advice from either of us."

"Well, that's just too bad," Tia said, "because this time he's going to have to."

"What are you going to do?" Andy asked.

"I'm not sure," Tia said. "But one way or another I'm going to make him listen to me. And he'll get to that audition tomorrow if I have to drag him there."

"Now, that I'd like to see," Andy said.

"Oh, go find your *pantalones*," Tia told him. She was going to keep Conner from throwing away his future for Alanna. She just had to figure out how.

Conner McDermott

Twenty-two-hundred miles. That would take me . . . damn. Close to thirty-six hours. And that's if I drive straight through.

Okay, so how about a bus? I could be there by Thursday. But by then Alanna could be long gone.

Flying is the only way. But who's going to give me the money? Evan? No way he's got that kind of money lying around. Liz? That's a joke.

Still, there's got to be a way. I just have to find it.

Time to Move On

Seven more classes, Ken thought, walking down the hall with Maria at his side. He wasn't sure he was going to make it. And what was the point anyway? It wasn't like he needed to keep his grades up just in case a prospective college decided to check him out. There weren't any colleges out there that were going to bother. Maybe he should quit high school too. That would give his father something to yell about.

Suddenly Maria stopped. "What's going on, Ken?" she asked, taking his elbow and leading him to the side of the hallway.

"Huh? Oh. Nothing," he said, glancing over her shoulder, at his feet, toward the freshman boy walking by. Anywhere but into Maria's eyes.

"Look at me," she said, gently touching his shoulder. "You've been dragging ever since you met with Mr. Nelson yesterday. What's going on?"

Reluctantly Ken gazed into Maria's dark eyes.

They were intense and demanding, but also full of concern. He shook his head, not wanting to let her know just what a loser he really was. Still, he was going to have to tell her sooner or later. He might as well cut her loose now and spare her the humiliation of still being with him when everyone else started to figure out why he wasn't getting any acceptance letters.

"I'm not going to college," Ken mumbled. "I can't."

Maria knit her eyebrows together. "What do you mean, you can't? Is it money? Because there are a lot of good financial-aid programs out there. You could—"

"It's not money," Ken interrupted.

Maria scrutinized his face. "What, then?"

Ken snickered. "It's kind of funny, actually. I mean, all this time I've spent agonizing over whether or not to take that football scholarship, where to go to school, how to tell my dad I'm not interested in playing college ball, writing all those essays." He chuckled to himself, but Maria just wrinkled her nose.

"I don't get it. What are you talking about?" she asked.

"It's just kind of funny, that's all," Ken went on. "I mean, if anyone had ever bothered to look at

118

my transcript, they could have saved me a lot of trouble."

Maria leaned in closer. "Ken, you're going to have to spell this out for me. I still don't understand," she told him.

Ken raised his head and looked directly into her eyes. "I'm not going to college because I can't. I'm not qualified. I don't even have the basic math requirements, and it's too late to get them."

"You're kidding," Maria said.

"Nope," Ken answered. "Mr. Nelson told me yesterday. None of the schools I applied to will even read my application. They'll just look at my transcript, realize I'm missing a math credit, and start typing the rejection letter. So that's it. I'm not going."

"Ken," Maria said. "That can't be right. You must have heard him wrong. How could Mr. Nelson have made such a huge mistake?"

"It's not Mr. Nelson's fault," Ken said. "He just started this year."

"Still," Maria began, "someone should have noticed."

"Who? Mr. Tingley?" Ken said, causing Maria to wince. "He's the one who told me to drop geometry sophomore year and take accounting instead, and then he left. And I don't think I ever even met with a guidance counselor last year. Besides, up until September everyone thought I'd be going to school for football, so who cared what my transcript looked like?"

"Oh my God. This is horrible." Maria shook her head. "Well . . . what else did Mr. Nelson say? I mean, what are your options? What do you need to do next?"

"Get a job," Ken sneered.

"Ken, I'm serious. You can't give up just because of one math credit. You're a smart guy and a great student—I'm sure there's something you can do. Any college would be lucky to have someone like you, and there's got to be a way we can—"

"Okay, stop right now," Ken snapped. He'd been leaning back against the wall, but now he rose to his full height—just an inch taller than Maria—and glared at her. "Because I can't take another one of your pep talks. That's what got me into this mess in the first place."

"What?" Maria said, drawing back and staring at him wide-eyed.

"It's true," Ken insisted. "Before I got together with you, I knew where I belonged—on the football field. But you got me thinking that I could actually make it without football. You kept on telling me that—"

"Ken—you weren't even playing football when we started dating. You quit the team, remember?"

"Oh, great. So you think I'm a quitter too," Ken barked.

"What? Ken—you're not even making sense. Look, let's just go talk to Mr. Nelson and figure out—"

"Screw Mr. Nelson, screw college, and screw you. I'm sick of everyone trying to build me up and make me into something I'm not. The only thing that ever gets me is disappointed," Ken said, turning his back on Maria and storming off down the hall.

Alanna checked the clock on Jeff's bedside table. Four P.M. Lisa would be home from basketball practice soon, and hopefully she'd have some ideas about where else Alanna could stay.

After the close call they'd had yesterday afternoon, the two of them had agreed that it wasn't safe for Alanna to hang out in Jeff's room anymore. Lisa thought it was time to either bring her parents into it or call the Feldmans, but Alanna had refused both options. Getting parents involved meant going to boarding school, and that was something she wasn't going to do.

So finally she'd gotten Lisa to agree to help her

get settled in a new place and to give her at least until the end of the week to come up with a more permanent solution. Of course, by the end of the week Alanna was hoping to be far away from Chicago, but she had no intention of telling Lisa that. It was becoming increasingly clear that she couldn't trust Lisa to cover for her much longer.

Alanna heard the front door slam and Lisa call, "I'm home," just to make sure nobody else was. Of course, no one answered, and a few seconds later Alanna heard Lisa's footsteps padding down the hall.

"Hi. How was your day?" Lisa asked, closing Jeff's door behind her.

"Can't complain," Alanna said, though if she'd wanted to, she certainly could have. It wasn't exactly a festival of fun being cooped up in the Bresinskys' house, even if they did have seventy-five cable channels and a Jacuzzi.

"Good. Well, here's what I found out," Lisa said, wasting no time. She spread out her notebook on Jeff's bed and started reviewing everything she'd written down. "You could stay at the local YWCA, no questions asked, for fifteen dollars a night, although if you fill out some paperwork and sign some forms stating that you can't afford it, they might be able to give you a discount—like five or ten dollars a night or something like that. So that's the first option, and personally, I think it's the best one."

Alanna nodded. "I could do fifteen a night for a while," she said, calculating how long her father's money would last between that and meals. She didn't want to use the credit card anymore, having realized that when her parents got the bill at the end of the month, all of her charges would be listed right on it. So of course, they'd eventually realize she had bought a plane ticket to Chicago, but by that time she'd be gone. And there was no sense giving them any more information to go on. "What else is there?" she asked.

"A homeless shelter, which would be free, and you'd get your meals too, but . . . I don't know," Lisa said, hesitating.

"What?" Alanna asked.

Lisa lifted one shoulder. "I guess I just don't like the idea of you sleeping next to a bunch of drunks."

Alanna raised her eyebrows. *If you only knew,* she thought. "Yeah, well. Is that it?"

"Pretty much. Unless you wanted to try a hotel. But the cheapest one around is eighty-five a night plus tax, so I didn't really think that was an option."

"Definitely not," Alanna agreed. "But what about youth hostels or churches?" she asked. "Isn't that where students traveling around the country always stay?"

"There is *one*," Lisa said, "in the basement of the Congregational Church just down the road, but it's full tonight. They said they might have room tomorrow night and I could check back, but I don't think it's such a good idea."

"Why not?"

"Because my dad volunteers there on Thursday nights. He runs bingo in the vestry. And if he saw you . . ."

"I'd be on the next plane back to California."

"Exactly."

Alanna grabbed Lisa's notebook from the bed and rested it on her knees. Her options weren't great, but at least she had some. "All right. The shelter it is," she said.

"The shelter? Why?"

"Because it's free," Alanna said.

"But think of the people you'll be staying with," Lisa said, wrinkling her nose.

Yeah, maybe I'll see someone from rehab, Alanna thought. "I'll be fine," she said. "Besides, it's only for a few nights. Until I figure out what to do next."

"I guess," Lisa reluctantly agreed.

"So when do we go?"

Lisa checked her watch. "Now, I guess—before my parents get home."

124

"Oh. Right," Alanna said. She stood up from Jeff's desk chair and looked around his room, realizing she would probably never lay eyes on it again. She glanced around one last time to make sure she wasn't forgetting anything and noticed her picture of Conner still sitting on Jeff's desk. "Do you think your mom will notice this is missing?"

"Maybe. But by the next time she changes Jeff's sheets, she'll probably have forgotten all about it. So . . . are you ready?" she asked.

Alanna clutched the picture of Conner in her right hand and slung the duffel bag over her shoulder. "As ready as I'll ever be," she said.

"Okay, then," Lisa said. "Let's go."

"That was nice," Melissa said, separating her lips from Will's. They'd only been making out for five minutes, but for some reason Melissa had suddenly pulled away.

"Then stay a little longer," Will said, leaning toward her. Melissa put her arms around his neck and kissed him again, but not for long.

"I'd like to," she said, "but I have a ton of homework to do."

"Are you sure?" Will said. "My mom won't be home for another half hour."

"Mmmm," Melissa sighed as he kissed her, then

she started to giggle. "I would, Will, really. But I have two papers due tomorrow and a quiz to study for."

"All right," Will said, continuing to kiss her until finally Melissa stood up. She glared down at him jokingly, and he couldn't help laughing. Sure, he and Melissa had their problems, but they had their fun too.

"Oh—there was one thing I wanted to ask you about before I go," Melissa said, pulling down her gray V-necked sweater and straightening her skirt.

"Don't worry, I didn't give you a hickey," Will teased.

Melissa just shook her head. "It's about Aaron Dallas."

"Aaron?" Will asked. "Well, I hope he didn't give you a hickey either."

"*Will,*" Melissa chided him. "Be serious."

"Okay," Will said, forcing his mouth into a straight line. "What is it?"

"Well," Melissa started. "Cherie's got a major crush on him, and I told her I'd ask you what was up with him."

"What do you mean?"

"You know . . . is he interested in anyone?"

Will squinted. Wasn't Aaron the one who had referred to the last half of senior year as party time? And he'd also made some comment about how it didn't matter how many girls he dated or who they were because he'd be leaving for Florida State at the end of the summer.

"Will?" Melissa asked.

"What? Oh, sorry," Will said. "I was just trying to remember something Aaron said."

"Well—what about Cherie? I mean, do you think she has a shot with him?"

"Uh . . . I'm not sure," Will said, trying to be diplomatic. Girls didn't always seem to understand where guys were coming from, and he didn't want Melissa to get the wrong impression about Aaron. He was a good guy—he just wasn't interested in a relationship. "I guess I'd have to say . . . no. I mean, nothing serious anyway. Aaron's sort of . . . too busy for a girlfriend right now."

"Too busy?" Melissa asked, narrowing her eyes.

"Yeah," Will said with a shrug.

"What do you mean, too busy?"

"He's just got a lot going on. You know, with basketball, and college, and . . . oh, yeah," Will said, suddenly remembering their period-four class. "He's not doing so well in English either."

"Really?" Melissa asked.

"Yeah. Mrs. O'Reilly told him today that if he didn't turn in revised copies of three of his papers and start doing better on his quizzes and tests, he's not going to have a passing grade at midterm, which means he wouldn't be able to play in any of the basketball tournaments."

"Wow," Melissa said. "That's terrible. He's one of our best players."

"Yeah, well, he's pretty bummed too," Will said, pleased with himself for having remembered it. Now Melissa would understand and she could break it to Cherie without making Aaron look like a pig. "So you can see how having a girlfriend isn't one of his priorities right now."

"Yeah, I guess so," Melissa said, biting her lip.

Oh, no, Will thought. *She's not going to drop it.* "What are you thinking, Liss?" he asked.

"Well," Melissa said with a grin. "I'm pretty good in English."

"*Yeah,*" Will said. "Go on."

"So, maybe I could help Aaron edit his papers and even tutor him a little." Will narrowed his eyes. That couldn't be the whole thing. It lacked Melissa's usual slant—the part where she got something out of the deal. "And," Melissa continued, "while I'm tutoring him, I could put in a good word for Cherie. Then once he had his English grade under control again, maybe he'd consider going out with her." She smiled at Will and widened her eyes, obviously waiting to hear what he thought.

128

"Wow," Will said, genuinely amazed. "That's really . . . thoughtful." Granted, she did have ulterior motives for wanting to tutor Aaron, but for once they weren't self-serving.

"Thanks," Melissa said. "But do you think it will work?"

Will shrugged. "I don't know," he said. "I guess it could."

"Well, even if it doesn't, at least it will help Aaron stay on the basketball court," Melissa said, and again Will was struck by her lack of selfishness. Could Melissa actually be changing? After all these years it hardly seemed likely. Then again, maybe the whole Erika episode had put things into perspective for her. Maybe she'd finally realized that she couldn't go around manipulating everyone and that if she really wanted her friends and her boyfriend to stick by her, she was going to have to make an effort too.

"You know, Liss," he said, pulling her close and nestling his chin in her soft, brown hair. "I'm glad we're back together."

"Me too," Melissa said, resting her head on his shoulder.

"And even if Aaron doesn't go out with Cherie, I think it's really cool that you're trying to help her out. And him too."

"Thanks," Melissa said, giving him a gentle squeeze

around the waist.

It felt good to have her back in his arms—natural. And if Melissa really was trying to change, Will decided he could too. He was going to stop thinking about Erika Brooks, and he wasn't going to get distracted by girls like Jessica Wakefield. He and Melissa were solid again, and that was the way he wanted it to stay, which meant no more fooling around.

And no more stupid mistakes.

Maria Slater

Okay. I'm going to go over this one more time.

First Ken tells me he's not going to college, so of course, I ask him why. He tells me it's because he's missing a math credit. I suggest we go talk to Mr. Nelson to see what can be done, and he blows up at me for calling him a quitter.

Nope. It still doesn't make sense. I didn't call him a quitter. Did I? I don't even remember saying the word. But even if I did, he was angry before he started talking to me, which means it's probably not me he's upset about. Right? So then why am I the one he's yelling at?

All right. One more time.

First Ken tells me he's not going to college. . . .

CHAPTER

Desperate Times

Conner unfolded the square of paper that had been jammed in his pocket all day and punched in the numbers that were written on it.

"Hello?"

"Lisa—this is Conner again. I need to talk to Alanna."

"I told you," Lisa replied, her voice cracking, "I don't know where she is."

"Look—you can drop the act. I know she's there. You basically told me the last time I called. And as soon as I can find a way, I'm coming to Chicago to see her. But for right now I just want to know that she's okay, so put her on the phone, all right?" Conner waited for a response, but instead he heard a sound like Lisa was holding her hand over the receiver, followed by the sound of her blowing her nose.

"Lisa?" he asked. "Are you okay? Where's Alanna?" If anything had happened to her . . .

"She's not here," Lisa said, her voice muffled by a

133

stuffy nose. For a minute Conner thought she might have a cold, but when he heard the way she was sniffling, he realized she must be crying.

"What happened?" he demanded. "Where is she?"

Lisa blew her nose again, then returned to the phone. "She's okay. At least I think she is. She was when I dropped her off. But that place was awful, Conner. I can't stand the thought of her spending the night there with all those . . . people."

"What are you talking about?" Conner asked, clutching the receiver so hard, his knuckles were beginning to turn white. "Where. Is. Alanna?"

"She's at a homeless shelter in town," Lisa said. "I took her there this afternoon. It's the only place I could get her to go. I wanted her to stay at the YWCA, but she didn't want to spend any money. I just wish I could have gotten her to talk to my parents. I know they could help her, but Alanna made me promise not to say anything to them. She's afraid they'll call her parents."

"Yeah, well, I can see why," Conner said. "The Feldmans aren't exactly . . . the touchy-feely type. Look, you did the right thing. How far away from you is this shelter?"

"It's right in town," Lisa said. "It's only, like, five miles or something—a fifteen-minute drive with traffic."

"So, then, you can check in on her in the morning and make sure she's still there?"

"Yeah, I can do that on my way to school," Lisa said. "And I'm pretty sure she will be. She signed in for the night, and from what she said to me, she's planning to spend at least one more there while she figures out what to do next."

"Good. That should give me enough time to get there," Conner said, although he still had no idea how he was going to manage it.

"Conner, I'm really worried about her," Lisa said, her voice breaking between sniffles. "I mean, I know her mom and dad aren't the greatest—that's why I've been covering for her the last couple of days. But still, I don't think being out on the street is the solution."

"I know," Conner said, hoping that Alanna at least had the sense to stay put where she was. If she moved on again before he got there, he might never find her. "But try not to worry too much. I'm going to get a plane ticket and get there as soon as I can, and I promise Alanna's going to be all right. We'll figure something out."

"I hope you're right," Lisa said.

"I am," Conner assured her. "But if you hear anything new from Alanna before I get there, I want you to call me, okay?"

"Okay."

135

"Here's my number," Conner said, and he rattled it off to her. Then, after making her repeat it, he hung up and ran down the hall. Getting the Feldmans involved was out of the question. His own mother, on the other hand, might actually be able to help. At least with the plane fare.

"Mom!" he yelled, jogging down the steps into the living room, but she wasn't there. "Mom!" he called down the basement stairs to the laundry. No answer. *She was here a minute ago,* he thought. She'd said hello when he came in from school. He ran out to the kitchen and glanced out the door.

"Damn," he said, realizing that her car was gone. He spun around and looked at the kitchen table, and sure enough, there was a note.

Conner—
I've gone to pick up Megan from basketball practice. Back in a half hour.
—Mom

Shoot, Conner thought. He didn't have time to wait around. If he was going to get to Chicago before Alanna was gone, he had to move fast. He was just about to grab his car keys and go to Evan's house to see if maybe Evan *did* have any cash stashed away when he noticed his mother's pocketbook on the

136

counter. *She must have forgotten it,* he told himself, walking over to it.

A quick look into the open top confirmed his thought. Everything was in it. Her wallet, her checkbook, her glasses—everything. Which meant she didn't even have her driver's license. But it was her checkbook that Conner was having a hard time taking his eyes off. It would be so easy to take one check—just one—and write it out to himself for enough cash to get an airline ticket. And he knew he'd never get caught. He'd been able to forge his mother's signature since sixth grade. Hell, he'd been taking care of most of the bills back when she was drunk all the time.

He removed the checkbook from his mother's purse and felt its weight in his hand. What was the saying? *Desperate times call for desperate measures.* Would it really be such a bad thing? His mother would understand. Wouldn't she? And of course he'd pay it all back as soon as he could.

Conner slid his fingers along the leather cover and traced the stem of the little embroidered rose. It would be wrong, he knew, but Alanna's life was on the line. Who knew what would happen to her if she left Chicago?

"Sorry, Mom," Conner mumbled, opening the checkbook. "But it looks like this is my only option."

*　　*　　*

"Conner! What are you doing?" Tia yelled through the screen door.

"Jeez, Tia!" Conner said, dropping his mother's checkbook on the floor. "You scared me."

"Yeah? Well, you're freaking me out too," she said, flinging open the door and storming in. "I hope you weren't getting ready to do what it looked like you were getting ready to do."

Conner narrowed his eyes at her. "And just what was that?"

"Stealing money from your mother," Tia said, picking up the checkbook and waving it at him. From what she could tell, she'd gotten there just in time.

"So what if I was?" Conner barked. "Don't you care that Alanna is out on the streets right now? That she could be getting mugged, or raped, or moving on to someplace where we'll never find her?"

Tia drew back slightly, thrown by the degree of emotion in Conner's voice. Until now she hadn't realized just how important Alanna had become to him.

"Look," she said, placing the checkbook into Mrs. Sandborn's purse and taking a deep breath. "You're right. Alanna's in trouble. And if the two of us just stand here yelling at each other, we're not going to do her any good at all."

138

She watched as Conner's jaw muscles tightened and relaxed, knowing from years of experience with Conner that he was trying to get a handle on his anger. "So what do you suggest we do?" he snapped, but at least some of his edge had been taken off.

"I suggest we sit down and try to figure out what we *can* do—and that doesn't include forging a check and taking off to Chicago."

Conner closed his eyes and let out a heavy breath, but he didn't protest. Tia pulled out a chair at the table, and after a few minutes Conner did too. They sat facing each other silently for a moment while Tia waited for Conner to come down one more level on the anger scale, then she began.

"Do you know how worried your mother would be if you just took off after Alanna?" Tia asked.

"Can we save the lecture for later?" Conner countered.

"Fair enough," Tia said with a nod. "I just have one more thing I need to say, and then we can talk about how to help Alanna."

Conner glared at her across the table. "What?" he said flatly, and Tia could see that he was finally back down to his normal level of broodishness and nothing more.

"What the hell were you thinking!" she yelled,

reaching across the table and smacking him on the head.

"Ow!" Conner groaned, frowning at her as he rubbed the back of his head with one hand.

"Seriously, Conner," Tia said, sitting back down. "Stealing from your mother? Taking off for Chicago? Skipping your audition tomorrow? You've gone totally loco! You can't go giving up everything for this girl!"

"I'm not—"

Tia held up a hand to let him know she wasn't finished, and he cocked his head and glared at her. "Now, look," she continued. "I know how important she is to you, and yes—I do realize that she could be in serious trouble. But if and when you get her back here, what kind of help are you going to be facing forgery charges—and who knows what other charges if the Feldmans find out you knew where she was and didn't tell them—plus having no future except maybe some stupid degree at some ho-hum college all because you blew your big chance so you could run off to Chicago?"

Tia took a deep breath and let it out slowly, resting her hands on the table in front of her.

"Are you done?" Conner asked.

"Yeah. Pretty much," Tia said, feeling much calmer now that she'd gotten all of that out.

"Good. So, now that you've reamed me out, what do you suggest we do about Alanna?"

Tia squinted. "I'm not sure yet," she said. Conner leaned back in his chair, letting his head loll backward so that he was staring at the ceiling. "But I promise you this," she added quickly, then she waited for Conner's full attention. When he was staring her in the eye, she went on. "If you get up tomorrow and go to your audition, I will find a way to get you to Chicago to help Alanna."

"Look, Tee, I appreciate it, but I can't wait until tomorrow."

"Well, you're going to have to," Tia said. "Because the banks are closed, and you don't have any money. Besides—do you even know if there's a flight leaving for Chicago tonight?"

Conner blinked and stared at the table. Obviously, in all his rushing around to find the money for a plane ticket, he'd never even bothered to consult an airline schedule.

"Okay, then," Tia said, sensing she was only a few steps away from victory. "Let's get online and find out what the earliest flight is leaving tomorrow—*after* your audition—and I promise you, I'll get you on it."

"And just how do you intend to do that?" Conner asked.

"I don't know yet," Tia admitted, "but I'll come up with something."

"Something like five hundred dollars?" Conner asked.

"Sure," Tia said. "No problem. I'm a good fund-raiser. I sold the most Girl Scout cookies in San Mateo County when I was in fifth grade."

"I know," Conner said. "You made me and Andy buy half of them."

"Oh, yeah. I forgot about that. Well, anyway—don't worry about the money. I'll handle the plane ticket, and you'll be in Chicago before dinnertime tomorrow. Just get to that audition."

"Just get me on a plane," Conner said.

Tia nodded and reached her hand across the table. After a moment Conner slowly raised his and shook.

"Deal?" Tia asked.

"Deal."

Phew, Tia thought, thankful that Conner had finally agreed not to skip his big opportunity. *Now . . . how on earth am I going to get him to Chicago?*

Ken opened the kitchen door slowly, heaving a sigh of relief when he saw that the chairs around the table were all empty. No father, no newspaper, no stupid lectures to listen to. He had dropped his backpack onto the floor and was just about to see what was in the fridge when his father called to him from the living room.

Oh, great, Ken thought. *Just when I thought I was free.*

"Ken," Mr. Matthews called a second time. "Can you come in here for a minute?"

Ken trudged into the living room, dreading another confrontation with his father. After all the fighting they'd done already, the scene he'd had with Maria that morning, and the C-minus he'd gotten on his physics test, he wasn't sure how much more he could handle.

But when he walked into the room, his father—instead of sitting in his recliner folding up the twice-read newspaper—was seated on the floor, surrounded by papers. It didn't take Ken long to realize what they were. Most of them had his dad's name in the corner along with one course number or another, and they'd all been typed out on his dad's old Underwood typewriter. He knew because he recognized the type from all the times he'd played with it as a kid.

"Dad . . . what—?"

"Sit down for a minute, Ken. I want to tell you something." Ken did as his father said and took a seat on the plush, brown carpet. "These are all papers I wrote in college," Mr. Matthews said, sweeping his hand above the top of the pile. "Go ahead—look at one of them."

Ken leaned forward and took one from the stack. It was titled "Muhammad Ali: The Greatest," and judging from the first paragraph, he thought it was actually pretty good. But one thing struck Ken— there were notes all over the margin in red ink, and some of them were pretty harsh. Stuff like, *You call this college level? Try varying the verbs once in a while, making the language more colorful. No one wants to read boring writing, even if it is about an interesting subject.*

"Wow, that's pretty harsh," Ken said, not realizing he'd said it aloud until his father responded.

"Yeah. My dad wrote that."

"The paper?" Ken asked.

"No, the comment. In fact, he wrote most of them," Mr. Matthews said.

Ken lowered one eyebrow and glanced at his father, then picked up another paper. It too was covered with red ink, and many of the comments were just as biting. "Why?" he asked.

Mr. Matthews cocked his head. "I guess because he wanted me to succeed."

"So he criticized you?" Ken asked, failing to see the logic.

"Yes. Although I guess I'd say it a different way. I say he *pushed* me. And it was the best thing he could have done for me. It forced me to work twice as hard just to please him," Mr. Matthews said, staring at Ken as though he were trying to communicate some deeper meaning. Ken stared back at his father, lost at first, but then it hit him, and he almost laughed.

"Oh, no." Ken shook his head. "You can't just feed me some line about your old man and then expect me to turn around and thank you for calling me a quitter. Gee, thanks for helping me build character, Dad," he mocked, standing to leave.

"That's not what this is about, Ken," Mr. Matthews said. "Please stay. Hear me out."

Ken stood where he was and chewed on the inside of his cheek. "Okay. Go ahead. I'm listening," he said.

Mr. Matthews wrung his hands in his lap and breathed out slowly. "I wanted to show you these papers so that maybe you'd understand something about me," he said after a moment. "I know I've been hard on you, and it hasn't always been justified, but . . . I've only ever wanted to help you."

"And I'm supposed to get that from your old college essays?" Ken asked.

"Not just the essays," Mr. Matthews said. "My father's comments too. Your grandfather. I know you never met him, but he was a good man. A very stern man, but a good one. And if he hadn't kept at me the way he did, I never would have even gone to college. I didn't want to—I wanted to play football and forget about academics, but he forced me to study. He forced me to work hard—it was the only way I could ever get an ounce of praise out of him. He thought sports were useless—didn't see a future in them."

"And so you thought if you rode me the way he rode you . . . ," Ken started, but his father shook his head.

"I don't think it's that simple. I'm not sure I ever even thought about it that way. I was doing what I knew—what my father always did."

"Yeah, but you were doing it in reverse. I've been telling you for a couple of months now that I'm not interested in playing football in college, and you've been trying to get me on a team. You even bribed that scout to get me into U. Mich."

"I know," Mr. Matthews said, "and I know that wasn't the best move I've ever made, but you have to believe me, Ken. I was only trying to help you."

"Yeah, because you knew I couldn't do it on my own," Ken snapped. "So how's it feel to be right? Does it feel good?"

"You still don't get it, do you?" Mr. Matthews said. "How can I get through to you?"

"You have," Ken said. "I got your message loud and clear last night. I'm a disappointment and a quitter. You couldn't have said it plainer."

"Ken—you have to stop being angry for a minute and listen to me. Can you do that? Just for a minute?" Mr. Matthews asked. Ken folded his arms across his chest and stared at his father. "Okay," Mr. Matthews said. "Good. Bribing Krubowski was stupid—one of the stupidest things I've ever done. But it had nothing to do with my belief in your ability. I was just trying to buy you the shot I wish I'd had when I was a kid."

A tightness stretched across Ken's chest, and he was conscious of its rising and falling as he breathed. Was his father telling the truth? Ken wanted to believe it, but there were still so many things that didn't make sense.

"So you think I'm smart enough to go to college for something other than football?" he asked.

"Of course I do," Mr. Matthews replied.

"Then why were you asking that girl at UCLA if athletes got special consideration in their classes?" he asked, watching his father for the slightest hesitation.

"Because I never could have made it there," Mr. Matthews said. "Not while playing football too. And I guess I was still hoping that's what you were going to do—play college ball."

147

"But I told you months ago that I didn't want to," Ken protested.

"I know you did, Ken, and that's what I'm telling you," Mr. Matthews said, his voice slow and even. "I wasn't listening. I was too caught up in what I wanted for you to see what you wanted for yourself. But I'm listening now."

"Unfortunately, now it's too late," Ken told him. "I'm not even going to *get into* college, so I guess you can kiss that dream of yours good-bye."

"Look, Ken. I know you're angry with me, and I know we've still got a lot of stuff to work out, but you have to do one thing for me—just *one thing.*"

Ken frowned. "What?"

"Don't give up. Not now. Not because of all the stupid things I've done. I talked with Mr. Nelson again today, and he assured me he's close to working something out. College *isn't* out of reach for you, and if you'd just take the time to go talk to him, you'd realize that."

"Yeah, but . . . you're talking community college, right?"

"No, I'm talking about the schools you applied to. Maybe even UCLA—I don't know. That's the thing—*you* have to talk to Mr. Nelson to figure this out. There's nothing I can do."

Ken squinted at his father, and Mr. Matthews

held his gaze. "Do you think UCLA's still a possibility?" Ken asked.

"I don't know. You'll have to ask Mr. Nelson," Mr. Matthews said.

"What? You mean you don't know anyone there that you could bribe to get me in?" Ken couldn't help slipping in.

"Look, I told you—bribing Krubowski was obviously a mistake," Mr. Matthews said, "but I have to say, I still don't see why it's such a tragedy. People get into college that way all the time. It's how the world works. Do you really think the president's son was qualified to go to Yale? Of course he wasn't. He got in because his father was—"

Ken gritted his teeth as his father spoke until finally he couldn't take it anymore. "Dad," he broke in.

"Hmmm? What?" Mr. Matthews asked.

"Look, I'll talk with Mr. Nelson tomorrow, but you've got to do me a favor first."

Mr. Matthews furrowed his brow. "Sure. What is it?"

"Quit while you're ahead," Ken said. Then he went upstairs to call Maria.

Ken Matthews

To: <u>mslater@swiftnet.com</u>
From: <u>kmatthews@swiftnet.com</u>
Re: Sorry

Maria,
   I don't blame you for not wanting to talk to me. Your mom said you weren't home, but we've got a history quiz tomorrow, so I know you must be there studying.
   Anyway, I'm really sorry about this morning. I was way out of line. And you're right. I do need to go talk to Mr. Nelson. But right now I just want to talk to you.

<Delete message>

Forget it. This is lame. I can't apologize to her through e-mail. I have to do it in person. Besides, if she's really not home, she can't check her e-mail. And even if she is, she wouldn't be checking it tonight. She'd be studying

for that quiz. Which, come to think of it,
is what I should be doing too. After all,
if college is still a possibility, I should
probably avoid failing quizzes right
now.

CHAPTER 10
SHUT UP AND DRIVE

"Maria!" Ken called, rushing over to her locker.

She turned to face him and started to smile, then stopped and pressed her lips into a flat line instead. "My mom said you called last night. What's up?" she asked, eyeing him tentatively.

"So you were really out?" Ken asked, raising his eyebrows.

Maria scowled. "Of course I was. What? Did you think my mother was lying to you?"

"*No-o,*" Ken said. "I just thought you might be avoiding me. You know—because of the way I . . . talked to you in the hall yesterday."

"*Talked* to me?" Maria said, folding her arms across her chest.

"Okay . . . *yelled* at you," Ken said. "But that's what I wanted to talk to you about." Maria watched him with unwavering eyes. "I'm really sorry," Ken told her, returning her gaze. "And you're right. I *do* need to talk to Mr. Nelson."

Maria drew back slightly. "You do?"

"Yeah. I do," Ken said with a smile. "And as a matter of fact, I have an appointment with him right now. You want to come?"

"Really?" Maria asked, the corners of her mouth curving upward. Ken nodded. "Absolutely," she said, slamming her locker closed. "Let's go."

When they walked into Mr. Nelson's office, Maria was still beaming, but Ken was beginning to feel a bit nervous. What if his father was wrong? What if Mr. Nelson hadn't come up with any options for him?

"Ken," Mr. Nelson said, reaching out to shake his hand. "I'm glad you could make it. Will you be joining us, Maria?" he added.

Maria glanced at Ken, then Mr. Nelson. "Yeah, if that's okay," she said.

"As long as it's fine with you," Mr. Nelson answered, turning back to Ken.

"Yeah," Ken said, knowing he could use the moral support. "It is."

"All right. Why don't you sit down?" Mr. Nelson said, gesturing to the two chairs in front of him and taking his usual seat behind his desk. Ken and Maria took their seats—Maria sitting forward, her hands folded neatly on her lap, and Ken leaning back and slouching.

"I'll make this quick," Mr. Nelson said. "Ken, I know

the news I gave you the other morning was a shock, but as I mentioned to your father, I've been working on finding a solution, and I'm pleased to tell you that there is a way we can get past that math credit."

"There is?" Ken asked, moving forward in his chair. His heart began to beat more quickly at the news. "How?"

"Well, as I said before, it's too late to get into one of the geometry classes that started this semester. However, there is a class being offered as part of the summer-school program, and I've already run it past the admissions offices of all of the schools you applied to. They all agree that as long as you're registered for it, they'll accept it as a math credit—contingent on your passing the class, that is."

"That's great," Maria said, glancing over at him, but Ken wasn't so sure.

"Summer school?" he said, narrowing his eyes.

Mr. Nelson shrugged. "It's the only way."

"So *after* senior year, *after* graduation, I have to come back here and take another class?" Ken said, his shoulders slumping forward. Mr. Nelson nodded. *That sucks,* Ken thought. But at the same time it would be a whole lot better than living at home and bagging groceries for a semester. Or a year.

"So," Ken started, straightening his posture. "Where do I sign up?"

*　　　*　　　*

"When did you first become interested in music?"

Conner blinked. It was a tough question—not that any of them had been easy so far. The woman who had asked it watched him over the top of her spectacles, while the other four members of the panel looked on.

At first it had shocked Conner that so many people were there, but with a half hour of questions already behind him, he was starting to get used to it. He was even beginning to get used to sitting all alone in the middle of the expansive room with its hardwood floors, although he still jumped every time he caught one of his own movements in the mirrors that lined the wall to his left.

"Mr. McDermott?" the spectacled woman prompted after a minute had passed. "Would you like me to repeat the question?"

"No," Conner replied, shaking his head. "I'm just . . . thinking about it."

She nodded, her brown lips curving into a wide arc. "Take your time," she said in a raspy voice that Conner imagined was capable of belting out an impressive jazz number or two.

"Well . . . actually, I'm not sure," he answered finally. "I mean, I can't really remember ever *not* being interested in music."

His questioner cocked her head and narrowed her eyes. "Can you elaborate?" she asked.

"Sure." Conner nodded. He should have known. So far he'd been asked to elaborate on all but one of his answers, and that one had been a yes-no question. "See, when I was growing up, my dad always had music going—when he was around, that is." *Which wasn't much,* Conner thought, but he didn't say it. These people didn't need to know his life story.

"He was a big country-western fan," Conner continued, "so I heard a lot of Hank Williams, Johnny Cash, Chet Atkins—that kind of stuff. Not that my music sounds like any of theirs, but it did get me interested in playing the guitar pretty young."

The panel members nodded politely and scribbled notes on the clipboards they were holding while Conner gazed at the clock above the door. He'd been sitting there for forty minutes now. *I hope Tia's figured out a way to get me to Chicago,* he thought, wondering what Alanna might be doing at that precise moment. *Hopefully, staying put.*

"All right," the spectacled woman said, her voice shifting Conner's focus from the streets of Chicago back to his audition. She removed her glasses and let them dangle from a red beaded chain around her neck, then she smiled her warm, brown smile. "I don't know about you," she told him, "but I've had enough questions for now. Let's have some music." She nodded toward his guitar, which was propped in a stand to his right, and Conner realized she meant for him to play.

"Okay," he said, clearing his throat. He stood from his chair and lifted the guitar, placing its strap around his neck as he'd done countless times before. He thought about standing while he played, but it felt more natural to sit, especially since he'd been sitting on his bed every time he'd practiced the piece he was about to play. He strummed a few chords to make sure the guitar was still in tune and flexed and relaxed his fingers to stretch them out. Then, when he was ready, he glanced up at the panelists, most of whom were sitting back in their seats with their arms folded across their chests.

"Do you want me to just . . . start?" he asked, swallowing hard.

"Whenever you're ready," the tweed man answered.

Conner nodded and cleared his throat again. Playing a gig was one thing, but this was totally different. When he played for a crowd of people, it didn't matter whether or not they liked him, but what these five people thought of his music could affect his future.

Conner rubbed his palms against his jeans one

last time to remove the sweat that had begun to form. Then, with a deep breath, he began strumming. He messed up the first three notes and winced, but he forced himself to keep going. And after a few more phrases, the music began to flow more naturally. When he finally relaxed enough to close his eyes, he felt like he was back in his bedroom, alone with the music, and—as it always did when he played—everything else began to fade away. The music was all that mattered.

"How did the audition go?" Tia asked, catching up to Conner in the parking lot outside the recital hall where his audition had been held. He was leaning against his car, with his arms folded across his chest, and his bag was already in the backseat. Obviously he'd been waiting for a few minutes.

"Fine. How's my plane ticket?"

"It's coming," Tia said. "But we have to go somewhere first."

Conner narrowed his eyes. "Where?"

"To the Feldmans'," Tia said. As she'd expected, Conner's jaw dropped and he glared at her as though she'd completely lost it.

"What?" he snapped. "Why?"

"Look—you did your part, now I'm doing mine," Tia told him. "Just get in the car and drive."

Conner scowled at her and stayed right where he was. "I don't see how—"

"If you want to go to Chicago," Tia said in a slow, measured voice, "just shut up and drive." She stared into his green eyes, refusing to look away. Finally it was Conner who blinked.

"Whatever," he said, walking around to the driver's side. "But you'd better know what you're doing."

"Of course I know what I'm doing," Tia said, easing into the passenger's seat. *Let's just hope the Feldmans go along with it.*

The drive to Alanna's parents' house was silent until Conner parked alongside the curb and pulled on his emergency brake.

"Don't talk, just listen," Tia said to Conner, waving her index finger. "When we get in there, you're going to tell Alanna's parents where she is—"

"Not if—"

"*Listen,*" Tia repeated, raising her index finger again. Conner rolled his eyes at her, but he shut his mouth, so Tia went on. "They are the only people around who *a*, have the money to get you a plane ticket to Chicago, and *b*, might actually do it if you can manage not to tick them off."

"Do you really think they're going to fly *me* out to Chicago? Three days ago they thought I was hiding her. They don't trust me any more than they trust Alanna."

Tia chewed her bottom lip, thinking things over. "I don't think they would send you alone. But I think they might take you with them. And even if they don't, at least you know they'll go get Alanna and bring her back here where you can keep an eye on her."

Conner cocked his head.

"Hey—it's better than having her wandering around by herself halfway across the country," Tia said.

Conner fiddled with his key ring. "I guess," he said finally.

"Okay, then. Are you ready?" Tia asked. Conner nodded, and they both exited the car, walking silently up the brick path to the Feldmans' front door. Tia was about to press the doorbell when the door swung open.

"Conner," Mrs. Feldman said. "Has Alanna contacted you?"

"Uh, no," Conner said, glancing at Tia. Mrs. Feldman turned toward Tia as well, and when Conner didn't introduce her right away, Tia gave her a weak smile.

"I'm Tia, by the way. I'm a friend of Conner's, and I've met Alanna a few times too," she said, extending her hand. Mrs. Feldman nodded at her and gripped her hand in a limp, cold fish of a handshake.

"Come in," Mrs. Feldman said. "Jake," she called, stopping in the foyer, "Conner's here."

In a few moments Mr. Feldman came rushing in and walked straight over to Conner, virtually ignoring Tia. "Do you have any idea why Alanna would go to Chicago?" he asked, causing both Tia and Conner to blink rapidly.

"You know she's in Chicago?" Conner asked.

"Well, yes," Mr. Feldman said. "The police discovered she bought a plane ticket using her credit card. But I didn't realize *you* knew where she was."

Suddenly Mrs. Feldman jumped forward. "How long have you known?" she asked. "And why didn't you tell us?" Then she turned to her husband. "I told you he knew. I told you we couldn't trust him." Conner shook his head and was about to turn—presumably to leave—but Tia caught his elbow.

"Okay, hold on a minute," Tia said. "You're all worried about Alanna, and you all want her to get home safely, so let's just try to talk about this calmly."

Mrs. Feldman took a deep breath and twirled the pearl necklace she was wearing around her fingers. "What I would like to know," she said, almost—but not quite—clenching her teeth, "is how you found out where she was. I don't imagine you have access to her credit card, do you?"

"No. I don't," Conner said, his voice cool.

Tia watched as he and Mrs. Feldman eyed each other like two cougars competing for territory. "Actually, Conner managed to track down one of Alanna's friends who lives in Chicago," Tia explained, gripping Conner's elbow tightly just in case he had forgotten that the Feldmans were his only hope for a plane ticket.

Mr. Feldman creased his forehead. "Alanna has friends in Chicago?" he asked, turning to his wife.

Mrs. Feldman shook her head. "Not that I know of," she said.

"Um, what is her friend's name?" Tia asked, prompting Conner to speak.

"Lisa. Lisa Bresinsky," Conner muttered.

"The Bresinskys!" Mrs. Feldman cried. "Of course! I'd forgotten all about them. But why didn't they call us?"

"They don't know she's there," Conner said.

"How could they not know?" Mrs. Feldman said, narrowing her eyes at Conner.

"Because she's staying at a homeless shelter," he said.

"A homeless shelter!" Mrs. Feldman yelled, her

eyes wide. "Jake, we've got to get her home."

"I know, I know," Mr. Feldman said. "I'll call the police and tell them to start looking near the Bresinskys' neighborhood—"

"The *police?*" Conner said. "Oh, man, if you have the police haul her back here—"

"And just what do you suggest we do?" Mrs. Feldman snapped. "You're the reason she ran away to begin with! If she hadn't skipped the charity auction to go to your foolish dance, we never would have—"

"*Me?*" Conner said, leaning closer. "You're the one who treats her like—"

"Hold on, hold on," Tia said, stepping between them. "This isn't going to get Alanna home."

"Neither are the police," Conner sneered.

"At least they were able to tell us where she is, which is more than I can say for you," Mrs. Feldman said, pointing an angry index finger at Conner.

"All right, all right," Mr. Feldman said, stepping forward. "This young lady . . . ah—"

"*Tia.*"

"Tia, yes." Mr. Feldman nodded. "Tia is right. Bickering isn't going to solve anything, and this certainly isn't the time for laying blame. Right now the most important thing is getting Alanna home safely. However, short of involving the police, I'm not sure how to do that."

"Conner has an idea," Tia said, then she turned to him. "Go ahead. Tell them."

Conner glared at her for a second, then reluctantly turned back to the Feldmans. "I think we should fly out there and get her."

The Feldmans exchanged a look, then turned back to Conner. "The three of us?" Mrs. Feldman asked. "Together?"

"Yeah," Conner said.

Tia waited for him to go on, but apparently he was done talking. "See," she jumped in. "If Alanna's at a shelter, you'd have to go in and get her, right? And so would the police. But chances are, she'd see you—or them—first." The Feldmans nodded, but they didn't seem to get the point. "Okay. So, if she saw the police or you two coming through the door," Tia continued, "no offense, but . . . well, she probably wouldn't stick around, would she?"

Mrs. Feldman narrowed her eyes again, and Mr. Feldman's posture stiffened, but neither of them denied it.

"But if she saw Conner," Tia went on, "well . . . after she ran up and hugged him, she'd probably listen to him. Plus there's this Lisa person. She's the only one Alanna's been in touch with, and she's the only one who really knows where Alanna is. And if she hasn't told her own parents that Alanna's around, she's probably not going to point you in the right direction either. Right? But she's been talking to Conner."

Tia turned from Conner to Mrs. Feldman, and finally to Mr. Feldman, waiting for someone to talk.

"She has a point," Mr. Feldman said finally, speaking quietly to his wife.

Mrs. Feldman twirled her pearls and sighed. "All right," she said. "We'll all go. I'll arrange the tickets."

Alanna Feldman

The woman in the bed next to me snores, and her breath smells like alcohol. Jack Daniels, I think. It was never my favorite, but it always calmed me down. After a few shots my hands would stop shaking and I could feel its warmth in my throat.

I don't know about this place. I mean, the meal wasn't too bad. It was chili— I picked all the beans out, and there wasn't much meat, but the sauce part was okay. The people are depressing, though. Some of them seem like regulars. They stand around and talk, and you can tell they all know each other pretty well. But there are others— like the woman sleeping next to me— who just wander in right before the doors close and sign up for a bed.

She doesn't look that old. Late twenties, maybe. I wonder how she ended up here—how anyone ends up in a place like this.

At least for me this is only temporary. I'm just staying here till I can figure out what else to do, and then I'll find somewhere else.

Because I definitely don't belong here.

CHAPTER 11

All's Well That . . . Ends?

"Can I get you something to drink?" the flight attendant asked. Conner watched as Mr. and Mrs. Feldman turned to stare at him.

"Yeah," Conner said with a nod, "ginger ale." The attendant smiled and started pouring, and the Feldmans went back to their magazines. *As if I'd order something alcoholic,* Conner thought, glancing sideways at Alanna's parents. They were unbelievable.

Back at the airport, just before they'd gone through airport security, Mrs. Feldman had started giving him instructions about exactly how to do it. "You need to remove everything metal from your pockets and put it in the little bowl before you walk through," she'd told him. About ten times. And she'd also informed him that if he carried a Swiss army knife or anything like that, he was probably going to lose it, so he might as well throw it away in advance and save them all the trouble.

Finally she'd admonished him to look the security

guards in the eye and smile so they wouldn't find him suspicious, and that's when Conner had lost it. He'd just glared at her and said, "I've flown before. I think I can handle it," and they'd barely said two words to each other since.

Now they were stuck in row four together—three seats, side by side—for the next three hours. Conner took a sip of his ginger ale and stretched out his legs. At least it was business class.

Mr. Feldman was seated next to Conner, who was on the aisle, and Mrs. Feldman had the window seat. So far, they'd been occupying themselves with various airline magazines, but Mr. Feldman appeared to be done with his. He folded it and placed it in the pocket on the back of the seat in front of him, then he turned to Conner and smiled. Actually, it was more like the corners of his mouth twitched, but it still seemed to be a gesture of goodwill. Kind of.

"So, Conner," he began, obviously feeling the need to make conversation. "What are your plans for after high school?"

"Plans?" Conner asked.

"Yes. What do you intend to do with your life once you graduate?" Mr. Feldman reiterated.

"Oh. Well, college, I guess," Conner said with a shrug.

Mr. Feldman gazed at him for a moment, then widened his eyes. "Can you elaborate on that?" he asked, which, in spite of everything, made Conner chuckle. "What is it?" Mr. Feldman asked, furrowing his brow.

"Nothing," Conner said. "It's just . . . I had an interview today, and there was this one woman who kept saying that." Mr. Feldman shook his head, clearly still puzzled. "You know, 'Can you elaborate on that?'"

"Oh. I see," Mr. Feldman said, nodding. "What kind of interview? Are you applying for a job?"

"No. School," Conner answered. Mr. Feldman held his gaze and waited, until it seemed like they'd been staring at each other for an unnaturally long time. Finally, if only to get Mr. Feldman to look away, Conner decided to elaborate on his own.

"College, actually," he said. "I had an audition for Belmont, a performing-arts school in Boston."

"Really?" Mr. Feldman asked, leaning forward slightly and shifting so that he was facing Conner a bit more squarely. At that point Mrs. Feldman turned to listen as well. "I've heard good things about that school. Do you know which one he's talking about, Joanna?"

"Yes, I think I do. Isn't that where Judy McCann's daughter goes? The one who was so magnificent in all of her school plays?"

171

"I think you're right," Mr. Feldman said. "And Judy raves about it, doesn't she?"

Mrs. Feldman nodded—toward her husband and, to Conner's surprise, at him. "Yes, she does. She says it's outstanding—rigorous standards, excellent professors. Was your interview an audition as well?"

"Yeah," Conner said. "I had to play a few things."

Mrs. Feldman widened her eyes and gazed at Conner again, scanning his face as if she were seeing it for the first time. "You must have had a good application. From what I hear, they don't grant those to just anyone."

"Oh," Conner said, unable to come up with anything else. It was the closest Mrs. Feldman had ever come to giving him a compliment. Actually, it was the closest she'd ever come to saying anything nice, as far as he could tell.

"My grandfather was musical," she went on, but she was gazing out the window now—almost talking to herself. "He could play the piano, guitar, saxophone—anything he picked up. And he could sing too. I always wished I'd inherited some of his talent, but it seems to have passed me by. I can't even whistle. Alanna, though . . . she has a beautiful voice. Sang in the church choir until she was twelve, but then . . ."

She closed her eyes and dropped her chin to her

chest. After a moment her shoulders began to shake, and Conner saw a tear roll down her cheek. Mr. Feldman put his arms around her and held her close, and Conner looked away.

"It's okay," he heard Mr. Feldman whisper, even though he was trying not to eavesdrop. Still, it was hard to give people their privacy when you were packed into a row with them on an airplane. Even if it was business class.

"She's going to be fine," Mr. Feldman murmured. "We're going to get her home safely, and everything's going to be okay."

Conner removed a magazine from the pocket in front of him and reclined his seat as much as possible. He tried to read an article about Puerto Rico's beaches, but he couldn't concentrate. No matter what he did, he couldn't get away from the sound of Mrs. Feldman's hushed sobs and Mr. Feldman comforting her. And he also couldn't stop thinking about what Mrs. Feldman had said. Alanna had a beautiful voice? She'd never mentioned to him that she'd sung in a church choir—or that she sang at all. Apparently there were a few things he didn't know about Alanna.

"It's going to be okay," Mr. Feldman's voice came again. He was repeating it over and over to calm his wife, who was still sobbing.

173

And maybe there were some things he hadn't known about Alanna's parents too.

"Aaron, hi," Melissa said, falling in next to him as he passed her locker. "Are you headed to English?"

"Uh . . . yeah," Aaron said, glancing at her sideways.

"Me too," Melissa said, "with Mr. Collins. You have O'Reilly, right?"

"Yeah. I'm in Will's class."

"I know," Melissa said, quickening her pace to match Aaron's gait. For some reason, Melissa had always thought he was shorter than Will, but now that she was walking right next to him, she realized he had to be at least an inch or two taller. And his eyes were bluer than she had thought too.

"Will mentioned that you were having a hard time," Melissa said. "With English, I mean."

"He did?" Aaron asked.

"Yeah," Melissa said. "Probably because he thought I could help you out. English is my strongest subject—I love to write."

"Really?"

"Mm-hmm," Melissa said, smiling up at him. "And I'd be happy to help you out," she added.

Aaron stopped suddenly and stared down at her. "Are you serious?" he asked.

"Yeah," Melissa said. "And I know I could help you get A's on all of your papers."

Aaron shrugged. "All right."

"Great," Melissa said. She flashed him a big smile. "So when do you want to get started?"

Conner slowed down when he saw a line of people standing along the side of the building on the block where Lisa had told him to look. It was a meal line—these people were waiting for dinner. *This must be the place,* Conner thought, walking up to the entrance. Once inside, the meal line curved off to the right, into a room that was filled with tables and chairs. Conner went to the left.

He walked down a narrow hall, past two rest rooms, and found himself staring into another room filled with beds and cots. Most of them were empty, so it didn't take him long to spot Alanna lying on hers, curled into a ball.

"Alanna!" he called, rushing toward her.

Slowly she sat up, rubbing her eyes and staring. Then finally she seemed to see him. "Conner!" she yelled, standing from her bunk just in time for him to wrap his arms around her.

"I've been so worried about you," Conner murmured into her curly brown hair, and just at that moment she slumped forward so that he had to catch her weight. "Are you okay?" he said, steadying her by grasping her shoulders.

"I don't know," Alanna said, the tears beginning to flow down her cheeks. "I don't know anything anymore. I just know I'm so glad to see you."

Conner pulled her close again and held her tightly. It had only been a few days, but already she seemed thinner, more fragile.

"I haven't had a drink," Alanna said, leaning back to look in his eyes. "I've wanted to so badly—especially last night, when this woman came in. She smelled like whiskey, and I just lay there wishing I had something to drink, but I didn't do it. I didn't even try. I promise," she said, her eyes pleading with him.

"I believe you," Conner whispered. "I do. It's okay," he said, smoothing her hair with his hand and holding her tightly. "It's okay. You're going to be all right."

"I'm just so scared," Alanna said, sobbing into his chest now. "I don't know what to do. I can't go home—they want to send me away, and I won't make it, I know I won't."

With every word Alanna said, Conner tried to hold her a little tighter. He wanted to make her feel safe. He wanted to protect her. But all he could do was keep telling her everything was going to be okay and hope that it really would be.

"Come on," he said when her crying seemed to be subsiding a little. "Let's get out of here. I have a room at the hotel around the corner." Alanna nodded and picked up her duffel bag, holding to Conner's hand tightly as he led her out.

"I didn't even ask you," she said when they'd made it out to the street. "How did you find me?"

"Lisa," Conner said.

Alanna furrowed her brow. "But how did you find Lisa?"

"I called Marissa. She had Lisa's address and phone number."

At that, one side of Alanna's mouth curved into a half smile. "You're quite the detective," she said, squeezing his hand and leaning into him. She stood on her toes and gave him a peck on the cheek. "I have no idea what I'm going to do next, Conner, but somehow, now that you're here, I feel like maybe things really are going to be okay."

Conner nodded and swallowed hard as they entered the hotel. Soon enough, Alanna was going to realize that he hadn't done this alone, and when she did, he was pretty sure she wasn't going to be thanking him anymore.

"Room 266," Alanna read as Conner slipped the key card into its slot. "I've always liked sixes. Maybe that's a good sign, or—"

"Alanna!" Mrs. Feldman yelled as she swung open the door. Alanna froze. She turned to Conner, then back to her mother, then glanced over her mother's shoulder to see her father standing there too. This couldn't be happening—it couldn't be true. How could her parents—?

All at once she realized what was going on. "You set me up," she said, staring at Conner. "You came and got me so you could bring me back to them. How could you do this?" she asked, but Conner just stood there, speechless.

"I said, how could you do this?" she yelled, but still Conner remained silent.

"Alanna, calm down, for goodness' sake," her mother told her. "You're making a scene."

Alanna whirled to face her mother, tears already streaming down her face again. "A scene?" she yelled. "You're worried about a scene? That is so like you—always worried more about the appearance of things than what's actually going on. I've had it with you and your stupid country club and your stupid friends! I've had it with all of you!"

"Alanna, look. I—" Conner started, touching her elbow gently, but Alanna was so full of rage that she jerked it away and glared at him.

"I don't want to hear anything you have to say! I

don't care! I trusted you, and you betrayed me! Get out of here! Get out!"

"But Alanna, I just—"

"I told you to get out of here!" Alanna yelled, her voice already growing hoarse, but she didn't care. She could barely get in enough breath to keep yelling, and her vision was becoming blurry—whether from tears or from exhaustion, she didn't know. She only knew that Conner had double-crossed her, lied to her, and that she couldn't trust him anymore. She didn't ever want to see him again.

Without thinking, she began to reach out with her hands and push Conner away, then the pushing turned into hitting. "Alanna," her father said, wrapping his arms around her so that she couldn't punch Conner's arm anymore. "That's enough. Come inside and sit down and get ahold of yourself. Conner, maybe it would be best if you went back to your room for now."

Alanna pushed against her father and tried to struggle free, but she didn't have the strength, and instead she ended up collapsing into him. She saw Conner turn and walk away, then her mother closed the door to the room. All Alanna could do was sob, and at this point it didn't matter that her father was the one holding her. She just needed to cry, to let the emotion out, and since his arms were around her, she leaned closer and cried into his chest.

Gently Mr. Feldman eased her over to the bed, where he sat down on the edge with her. Mrs. Feldman came to the other side and sat close, though she didn't seem to know how to give her daughter a hug. Once she tried to put an arm around Alanna's shoulders, but then she took it off and clasped her hands in her lap instead.

When Alanna was able to slow her cries and bring her breathing back to normal, it was her father who spoke. "Alanna, we've been so worried about you," he said.

"I'm so glad you're safe," Mrs. Feldman added.

Alanna glanced at her mother, surprised to see that there were tears in her eyes. And her father too appeared genuinely distressed. She'd never seen them this way, and it was almost difficult to believe.

They were actually concerned about her.

WILL SIMMONS
7:02 P.M.

Messing around with Jessica was stupid. Messing around with Erika was stupider. So I'm done screwing up. After everything that's happened, I'm back with Melissa. Again. And this time she's really trying to make it good, so I'm going to work at it too. Maybe there's a reason we keep ending up together. Maybe that's just the way it's supposed to be.

Alanna's okay. She's never going to talk to me again, but at least she's okay.

When I got back to my room, the little red light on my phone was blinking, so I checked for messages. There were five, and they were all from Tia, making sure everything was all right. So, yeah, Alanna's never going to talk to me again, but at least I know that there is one person I can always count on: Tia.

MELISSA FOX

7:39 P.M.

To: cherier@swiftnet.com
From: mfox@swiftnet.com
Subject: Dallas—and I don't mean Texas

Cherie,

Guess what—I'm going to be tutoring Aaron Dallas! It was sort of Will's idea since Aaron isn't doing so well in English, but while I'm working with him, I'll definitely put in a good word for you and figure out where he stands.

Before you know it, you and Aaron will be the coolest new couple at SVH! I just know this is going to work out perfectly!

Talk to you tomorrow,

Melissa